Cover art designed by
Cover photography by Dean Schoeppner
Cover modeling by Nick Nesbitt
Author photo by Trenton Wayne Photography

Copyright © 2015 by Nate Granzow

Note: This is a work of fiction. While the names of some public figures, locations, and actual world events are real, the characters in these pages and their exploits are entirely fictitious. Any resemblance to actual persons, living or dead, is entirely coincidental.

ISBN-13: 978-1512154641
ISBN-10: 1512154644

Never think that war, no matter how necessary,
nor how justified, is not a crime.—*Ernest Hemingway*

1
The Heavens Are Displeased

Aleppo, Syria
June 2013

It was all very Old Testament in its finality. Fire had rained from the skies, the sun blotted out by a pall of atramentous clouds. We sinners had felt the wrath of God. The keening of distant jet engines played a mournful requiem, their woven contrails like white scars on the dim morning sky.

"Shukri?" I called, my voice weak, smoke throttled. I stumbled through the wasteland, bypassing corpses and human puzzle pieces, looking for my fallen friend. Assad's helicopters had done meticulous work. It was slow going, slogging through the fresh mud, the earth clumsily tilled by cannon and rocket fire. "Shukri, where are you, man?"

A groan. My eyes scanned the ruins for any living thing. Leaning against the blackened remains of our troop carrier—its spine broken and buckled, the doors hurled fifty feet away in the blast—rested a mutilated, twisting, moaning shell of a man. His body had been camouflaged, charred to the same soot color as the destroyed truck. He clutched a book to his chest, the Quran, probably. The leather cover had been carved out, the fringes still smoldering from the heat of the incendiary 30mm cannon round that had passed through and hollowed his core. I hesitated; I didn't have time to comfort him in his dying moments. I knew my friend had been wounded, and if I was to save him, I had to continue my search.

"Please, American," the wounded man called out to me.

Slowly, as though every muscle twitch brought on a debilitating electrical jolt, he dragged his rifle alongside him by its sling. His eyes, vivid white against the ash on his skin, pleaded. Have mercy.

I approached him. He would have been unrecognizable if not for the raised laceration on his cheek—a perfect match to the one I'd stitched closed the day before. I knew this man. I also knew what he wanted.

He gestured with his eyes to the rifle. Although he had let go of the book in his hands, it stayed in place; the heat and blood had glued its pages to his shirtfront.

"I can't," I croaked, shaking my head. "I'm sorry, I can't do that."

His fingers curled into pained fists. "Please," he mouthed.

I turned away. Nearby, a wooden crate of grenades had been overturned, the smooth, baseball-size explosives scattered atop the dirt like fallen pinecones. I picked one up and glanced back at the wounded man. He nodded. Squeezing the spoon, I pulled the pin and knelt beside him.

"You do it," I said, helping him lift his arm. I gagged as skin sloughed off in my palm. With the two remaining fingers of his left hand, he clutched the grenade to his gut. He gave a small nod and closed his eyes.

Should I offer my condolences? Some sort of benediction? What could a survivor say to a victim that wouldn't sound as though I was reveling in my own good fortune, or that wouldn't come across as a synthetic lamentation of his ill luck? So I didn't say a word. Instead, I ran until I heard the thump of the explosive, a whisper in the ear after the thunderous onslaught we'd endured. I hoped the grenade had done the job, but I couldn't go back to check. I still hadn't found Shukri, and there was an ominous electricity in the air telling me to clear out before the Reaper finished sharpening his scythe and came looking for me.

My name is Grant Cogar.
The world thinks I'm dead.
I'm not sure they're wrong.

2
A Journey Begins

Chicago, Illinois
August 2012

Like a pile of decaying viscera, I sat, feet up, in my underwear, doing my best to fuse with the couch cushions as I watched the second cycle of the day's news—or the third, I don't remember. The news ticker scrolled past at a leisurely pace, teasing a story about a typhoon in Taiwan. The shades were drawn, the apartment silent apart from the whir of a neighbor's vacuum on the floor beneath mine. Wherever my pants were, inside the back right pocket was a lonely, twice-folded twenty-dollar bill and a stack of credit cards sticky with debt. In the fridge rested two cans of cheap beer and a half-eaten slice of pork roast my elderly neighbor had insisted I take two days before. It had a smell I didn't trust. The geriatric, not the pork. I was ten pounds overweight, muscles and mind atrophied, coming down from a brief and unsatisfying caffeine high, feeling the sweat trickle down my bare chest and wondering if the air-conditioning unit duct taped to the window frame would run if I could afford to plug it in.

My apartment, that one familiar anchor in my otherwise chaotic life, had begun to close in on me. It had developed a dustiness without being dirty, a solitude without being uninhabited. It gave off the same sort of feeling one might get upon entering a derelict log cabin, a cast iron pan still suspended over a fire gone cold, a book left open on the table, boots by the door. All the inviting warmth of a stage set wheeled behind the curtain and left in the dark.

Maybe I should get a cat.

Two prosaic, local government-watchdog-type articles I had no ambition to finish sat half-written on my laptop: One, on hold until my FOIA request got fulfilled, was an investigation into a privacy breach at the Illinois Department of Veterans' Affairs. The other, a wandering piece with an uninspired lede and a dearth of credible sources, was about railway transportation of hazardous waste. Better prospects had failed to materialize, and it didn't look like any worthwhile assignments were on the horizon.

I finally convinced myself to go to the kitchen to reheat another cup of coffee in the microwave. I would have preferred whiskey. Today was the perfect sort of day to drink oneself into a state of drooling, passed-out-on-a-park-bench narcosis, but the kitchen cabinets were as empty as my wallet. Haphazardly flipping through the pile of mail on my kitchen table, I searched for an invite to some press event or grand opening that might have an open bar. I'd dust off a tux if it meant access to someone else's liquor cabinet. Those invites usually ended up pinned to the refrigerator and forgotten about. But the fridge was bare, the stack of mail empty of anything but solicitations and overdue bills.

I glanced at the television. They'd begun interviewing a Syrian refugee, a young boy. He looked right through me, panicked, bloodied, and mud-spattered, wearing that same lost, exhausted expression I'd seen a thousand times before in my travels to countries seized by the barbed jaws of strife and disaster. But this felt different. There was something accusing in his eyes, something that drove a stake of guilt through my gut just by looking at him.

Then it occurred to me: I'd always been the one behind the camera, the one delivering the story to the people back home, doing my part to bring attention to those who needed a voice. But now, I'd become my audience. And I'd already watched this newscast twice. And I hadn't noticed. I hadn't cared.

And that sickened me. I turned off the TV, got dressed, and went for a walk.

I spent the following day calling up old sources and my most dependable street urchins, entreating the news gods for some kind of story that would vanquish my boredom. Nothing. At the least convenient time, Chicago had become quiet and peaceful. But as I continued to hunt for a story, in the back of my mind, I kept envisioning that Syrian boy's eyes. They gnawed at me.

That afternoon, at a coffee shop where the barista kept giving me annoyed looks for not buying more than one small, seventy-cent cup of black coffee as I obstinately parked myself in a corner with my laptop, I felt a spark rising deep in my chest. The subtlest flicker, but it grew until, for the first time in months, I decided I needed to do something. Not as a journalist, but as a man. At that moment, I decided to get off my ass and go to Syria.

Even before I began doing my homework, I knew Syria was one of those holes in the world that journalists spoke to one another about in hushed tones. It was a dark place, a quagmire that drew men in and swallowed them whole. The civil war that had engulfed the country was one giant Gordian knot, the likes of which had left even seasoned intelligence operatives and international relations gurus scratching their heads in search of a good solution. Naturally, such a mare's nest was dangerous. And complex situations where bullets were involved usually meant hard work. No one likes hard work, least of all me. That said, I'd made up my mind. I was going, even if it killed me. Which, the more I read about the place, I believed it might. Still, it had to be better than languishing here.

With a few hours of research under my belt and a few inquisitive calls made to connections familiar with the country, I rang my editor. After I pitched the story idea, Kailas grudgingly agreed to give me an advance of about half of what I actually needed to fly to Turkey and bribe my way into Syria. So I caught the bus to the *Herald'*s offices, got my check, and checked out one of the paper's SLR cameras. I marched straight down to my local pawn shop with it and left clutching a wad of cash and an empty camera bag. They wouldn't miss it for months, by which time I would have forgotten I'd taken it in the first place. I bought my plane ticket that night.

At home, I stuffed my clothes and gear into my old leather duffel bag. The zipper never stayed closed, so I had to weave a twist-tie through the eyelet of the sliders to keep my clothes from ending up scattered throughout the plane's cargo bay. The bag itself had weathered the years about as well as I had—poorly, and bearing a patchwork of scuffs and scars to prove it. It was an unsightly thing, but it was like an old traveling companion. A lucky one.

I looked around my bedroom. The sheets, wrinkled and untucked, still smelled faintly of women's perfume. Tiffany? Tanya? Something like that. We hadn't spoken since she'd come over a week before, which was just as well. She was perpetually adjusting her underwear, which, though it turned me on at first, soon proved just an irritating compulsion.

The walls were empty except for one stretch of drywall where, after a bottle of tequila, I'd decided I needed to hone my knife-throwing skills with a set of steak knives. Dirty clothes I meant to wash a week before covered the floor. A quintessential bachelor's pad.

I'd always felt a sense of melancholy when leaving this place. It had been the only home I'd known. Every time I left it to travel abroad, I knew I might not return. One day, I'd face a marksman who knew how to lead his target, or a mortar crew who had mastered the art of bracketing, and I'd be sent home in a body bag. Now, staring at this barren place, I felt nothing. No attachment, no sense of ownership.

I might not make it back, and I wasn't sure that bothered me anymore.

3
Welcome To It

Aleppo, Syria
June 2013

William Tecumseh Sherman once said there is no use trying to reform war, as the crueler it is, the sooner it will be over. Sherman had obviously never visited the Middle East.

If he had, he would have known that there is no limit to the depth of human depravity, and wars in this part of the world don't come with expiration dates. The Middle East is an island buoyed by corpses, rocking unsteadily atop a bottomless lake of blood—a lake that Sherman only briefly canoed over during his stint as general. Here, every drop of red spilled in the sand fuels the strife like gasoline on flame. Increases its duration, its heat. The place is thirsty for it. Even in those rare moments where the fire appears to have gone out, the embers beneath the ash are glowing red hot, ready to erupt at the first taste of an accelerant. It's always been that way. The weaponry has changed, but the brutality has, at best, remained the same. The threshold for suffering in this place is so much higher than Sherman could have imagined; cruelty doesn't discourage the warmongers here, it incites them.

Why? Because after millennia of genocide and barbarism, violence is no longer shocking. It's just business.

"*T'hamil bnadq. Ayzeen rasas kaman.*" A gaunt Free Syrian Army soldier, bearing a jagged cut on his cheek from a shrapnel wound he'd acquired the day before, moved down the line handing out ammunition. He stumbled as our ponderous troop carrier rolled over a mortar crater. Regaining his footing, he shoved an AK-47 magazine under my nose and shouted, "Where are your magazines? You need more ammunition, American."

I bumped the plywood stock of my Chinese Type-56 rifle with my fist and replied, "I've got plenty here, thanks. I'm very selective about when I shoot. Besides, I've got a sensitive shoulder and I'm pretty sure I'm allergic to gunpowder. Makes my throat tight and my ass break out in boils. It's pretty painful."

Looking away with disgust, the soldier continued down the line.

"Try to keep that bit about the boils between the two of us though, eh?" I shouted after him.

For ten months, I hadn't fired a single round of ammunition. I'd only begun carrying an empty rifle to keep the others from asking questions about what I was doing there. Such inquiries made me uncomfortable, since I still wasn't quite sure *what* I was doing in Syria. I'd given up on the notion of reporting months before, had stopped checking in with my editor altogether—Kailas had probably written me off for dead by now anyway—and spent my days following around an eclectic gallimaufry of rebel forces from all over the Middle East.

One thing I was sure of: I wasn't there to fight, even if I looked the part. Sporting the longest, most unruly beard I'd grown in my life, I wore a pair of blue jeans so dirty they looked brown and an old camouflage jacket that had doubled as my pillow since the day I'd arrived. The relentless Syrian sun had darkened my skin so much, if it weren't for my grain-colored hair and blue eyes, I might have passed for someone of Middle-Eastern descent without much scrutiny. To those outside my platoon, I usually just lied and said I was a Chechen, anyway. Nobody seemed to care enough to challenge me. I was here, they were here, and since we weren't shooting at each other, we must be on the same side. Today.

My stomach grumbled. Either the nervous anticipation of another rough day or indigestion.

Probably both. Scraping my rifle's buttplate against the truck's steel bed as we jostled along the artillery-pocked road, I looked out over the desolate landscape surrounding the city of Aleppo. The smoldering carcasses of cars and livestock stippled the ground. The distant city chattered with subdued gunfire, punctuated by the muted concussions of falling artillery.

Dust. If I could choose only one word to describe what the country had become, it was dust. The subdued, unvarying color of the crumbling buildings—like sand and decaying leaves—the thick, polluted haze that obscured the distance and made the air hard to breathe, the piles of rubble scattered errantly in the middle of streets or where buildings once stood; the word was fitting. It was as though the essence of life had been drained from the city, and all that remained was a shriveled, mummified corpse.

Syria never really stood a chance. Conquered by the Byzantines, Ottomans, English, and French before transitioning to a couple of nepotistic authoritarian dictatorships, the country was just one of those cursed with ill luck from the moment it was conceived. In a nation the size of Spain, only a tenth of its land was arable. The rest was just desert and looming mountains. Leading up to the civil war, the country had suffered a five-year-long drought comparable in severity to the American Dust Bowl in the 1930s. Sweltering temperatures, no rainfall, what little topsoil there once was swept away. There was no work to be had and no natural resources to export. It left Syria overpopulated, underemployed, and with a nasty reputation for violence known throughout the world.

"What do you think, Mr. Cogar? Seems like a good day to die, doesn't it?" My friend, a Syrian doctor named Shukri Faizel, meek and slight of build, peeked at me over the rims of his glasses. Sniffing the air thoughtfully, a mousy smile swept across his face and he continued, "You and me, we'll go see Allah today, what do you say?"

I winced and shook my head. "I actually had plans for today. Got to pick up my dry cleaning and do some grocery shopping. Tomorrow would work better, if you're free."

This had become our daily routine. We joked about death as though it were nothing, because if we didn't, its presence would consume us like an acid—nibbling away at the edges until there was nothing recognizable left. It was a desperate attempt to cling to sanity by embracing the insanity of it all. We both knew one day the jokes would come true.

A sudden cacophony of heavy machine gun fire and the *boom-wish* of a rocket-propelled grenade triggered close by interrupted our truck's diesel drone. Instinctively pitching over our vehicle's side and rolling to the ground, I slid into cover inside a deep hole still smoldering from the payload of a Skorpion anti-tank missile.

From the road, Shukri peeked into my hiding place and extended his hand toward me.

"Come, Mr. Cogar, we've work to do."

"But, the gunfire...."

"Ours. Rebel ambush up ahead. We've got injured to tend to."

That was Shukri's way of politely saying we'd be spending the next hour wading through dead bodies to get to the few injured enemy soldiers still intact enough to save, only to have to drag them through a crowd of bloodthirsty onlookers standing around the scene like voyeurs at a '70s sex party, palms sweaty, pupils the size of golf balls.

What happened to those prisoners after we saved them was up to speculation. Any time I asked about it, I was told they went away to rebel-held prison camps, but no one could ever seem to recollect seeing one or could tell me where they were located. Something told me those prison camps were probably in the same imaginary place as the farm everyone's childhood pet gets taken to when they get old. Why would the rebels bother keeping them alive? It was common knowledge that Assad didn't negotiate for prisoners. Soldiers on both sides of the fight knew that being taken alive meant far worse than being killed in a firefight.

Following the medic to where the skirmish had occurred, I watched helplessly as a bearded rebel wearing all black stripped the shirt from a captured regime soldier. Shouting the Takbir and raising a knife in the air defiantly, he plunged the blade into the man's belly. The dull smack of the blade as it struck flesh, and the screams that followed as the executioner forced the knife further into the screaming man's chest cavity, made me heave. I bit down on my fisted hand and pinched my eyes shut, willing the vomit back down. The jihadist cut free the soldier's still-pulsing heart. Stuffing the organ into his mouth and chewing it like a dog would a fresh bone, the Islamist grinned at his companion, who pointed a small video camera at the spectacle. Another low-budget propaganda film in the works. It was that kind of barbaric conduct that kept the world from empathizing with the Syrian rebels, seeing even the moderates in the FSA as insane by association. The jihadists fought against Assad—the common enemy—but it was just another case of "the enemy of my enemy is my friend."

And these guys didn't make good friends.

"ISIS?" I asked Shukri.

"I overheard them talking," he replied, trying hard to keep his eyes locked straight ahead, away from the scene of the soldier's execution. "They're with Nusra. Best if you avoid them, Mr. Cogar. I doubt very much that they would find you as endearing as I do."

I stuffed a fresh ya-dom stick inhalant—one of a large supply I'd purchased from a street vendor in Turkey for use as bribes at checkpoints—up my nose and breathed deep the sharp, medicinal scent of camphor and menthol. It shut out the smell of putrefaction and settled my stomach.

"Wait, please. I'm not with the Syrian army, I'm an American!"

My blood ran cold. Tilting my head toward the familiar voice, I spotted him. A stocky, middle-aged Indian man had been driven to his knees, hands in the air, with half a dozen rebel soldiers pointing their weapons at him. He had the looks of a man who'd been sent on an unexpected business trip to a region he'd never even read about, and certainly didn't pack for.

I whispered, "Kailas?"

4
An Adventure in Spades

Of the many people I'd met in my life who I would have gladly dragged into one of the bloodiest war zones I'd borne witness to in my career, my mentor wasn't one of them.

"I want to ask you what you're doing here, but I'm afraid you'll tell me you came just to see me," I said, waving off the soldiers as I helped him to his feet.

"Want me to lie to you and say I just swung by on my way to the post office?" Despite his nonchalant sarcasm, Kailas's eyes were wide, his face covered in beads of sweat. He was terrified, as well he should have been. Had I not been on that exact truck that had rolled in at that exact moment, he would have been executed and I never would have known. I would have walked past his body without giving it a second glance.

He continued, "I got a package in the mail with that ratty leather duffel bag of yours inside and a letter saying you were still alive in Aleppo, so I came to rescue your sorry ass."

I scowled, though I was pleased to hear that my venerated AWOL bag had survived. It'd been confiscated upon my arrival with the rebels, and I immediately set to work thinking of who could have sent it, and that letter, to my editor. Shukri patted my back and pointed to a wounded soldier nearby before leaving us.

Suddenly remembering the ya-dom stick poking out of my nose, I tugged it free and said, "You might just be the last person on earth I'd nominate for a one-man war-zone extraction, Kailas. You've been out of the U.S. what, twice in your life? And that was to vacation in southern Europe and the Caribbean. This is a little outside your skill set, Rambo. Besides, I don't need rescuing."

"You ungrateful bastard. I flew for two days and crawled through miles of sewer lines to get into this country."

But his clothes didn't look it. They were as crisp, pressed, and tidy as if he'd just stepped out of his front door back home in Chicago. That didn't surprise me: Kailas had always been an adamant believer that clothes made the man, and had, from the day I met him, insisted I dress like a professional whenever possible. I usually met him halfway. More or less.

"I'm not ungrateful. I'm happy to see you," I said, softening a little. "But I also know that of all the kidnappings and near-misses I've had—and there have been many—you've never once considered hopping on a plane to come bail me out. In fact, I recall a certain instance in Shanghai where you hung up the phone on my captor and nearly got me killed."

"Oh come on, I thought that was a prank call. Not as though you haven't made those kinds of calls before. You remember the stripper incident of '03? I get a call on my home phone at two in the morning from some pimp named 'King', saying he had you strung up and wanted his Elvis costume back—"

"I remember, Kailas," I interrupted, running a hand through my hair as I watched a line of men dragging corpses into a pile.

"Besides, the difference between Shanghai and now is a matter of you falling off the grid for ten months," Kailas continued, dusting off his dry-clean-only white shirt and staring indignantly at the rebel soldier who'd sullied it by pushing him into the dirt. "Everyone stateside thought you'd been killed in action or had been taken prisoner. We requested a media blackout and had the State Department looking into your disappearance, for Chrissake."

He was lying. No one knew or cared that I'd been gone. I had no family, few friends, and as a rule, the

U.S. government tried to keep kidnappings of their citizens quiet to prevent the kidnappers from thinking their victim was worth a ransom, and to keep the public from protesting their inaction. The *Herald* might have initiated a news blackout had I been higher profile or if they'd had some idea of who had kidnapped me, but since I wasn't and they didn't, they'd probably just passed around one of those ambiguous internal memos noting my absence and saying something to the effect of "we're pursuing all possible options" before standing by to see if my body washed up. Those media blackouts were bullshit, anyway; no one was ever saved by silence.

None of it really mattered. I was fine. Certainly better off than others in the industry. I knew of a dozen journalists, nearly all of them freelancers like myself, rotting away in musty cells from Vietnam to Iran, and few besides their immediate families and a handful of Defense Department officials had a clue. There had been several reporters here in Syria that had gone missing just since my arrival. We all knew the risks, but none of us, especially freelancers without the support of large media companies, held illusions about our perceived worth to our countrymen. On good days, we were ignored. Bad days, people wished far worse on us than simply being kidnapped.

Kailas continued. "When I got word that you were here, alive, I knew it wasn't like past times, so I came to bring you home myself."

I scanned the faces of the FSA soldiers milling around, all of them trying to decipher what our conversation was about and what this nicely dressed foreigner was doing standing in the middle of a bloodstained farm field.

I cleared my throat and said, "Let's continue this conversation on the road. We probably shouldn't stay here long."

Kailas didn't argue. As he stepped toward me, one of the Nusra militants, all but his eyes, challenging and feral, hidden by a checkered keffiyeh, emerged from the crowd and planted a hand on my mentor's shoulder, wrenching him backward. The man planted the barrel of his stockless AK-47 against Kailas's neck.

Typically, when deciding whether to fight a man or run from him, I sort through a mental checklist. If my opponent has tattooed knuckles, a nose that looks like it's been broken more than once, cauliflower ears, and finally—most importantly—a weapon in his hand, it's time to vacate the premises. But there was no running away this time.

Raising my rifle to my shoulder, I screamed to let Kailas go.

Yeah, my empty rifle.

My shouts were lost in a sudden uproar as FSA soldiers and jihadists faced off, guns bristling, with me, Kailas, and Kailas's new best friend in the middle of the action.

As quickly as it started, the shouting stopped. An eerie silence befell the battlefield. No one moved, their guns trained on the opposition. Even the artillery, an omnipresent noise in Aleppo, had fallen silent. I felt a bead of sweat trickling down my hairline heading for my left eye socket. I licked my lips and rolled the dice.

The butt of my rifle still buried in my shoulder, finger on the trigger, I stepped toward Kailas, extending my left hand toward him. The jihadist shifted his rifle from my mentor's neck, aiming it at my face as I neared. Staring down that black bore, that tunnel of death, I gripped Kailas's wrist and tugged him toward me. I took a much-needed breath as the jihadist relinquished his grip. We backed away slowly, returning to the relative safety of my men.

The militant snorted, moving his pistol across his chest, and turned away.

It's a calculated risk to point a gun at an armed man. It's just bad mathematics if your gun is empty and the guy you're pointing it at is a religious fanatic who's probably killed more people before his balls dropped than most military contractors do in their entire career.

"Cogar, can we leave now?" Kailas asked, staring after the group of jihadists as they walked away.

"Without doubt the best idea you've had this week," I said as we headed back to the convoy. Pulling a piece of dried goat jerky from my pocket, I dusted the lint from it and offered it to my mentor. He looked at it dubiously and declined. Stuffing it in my cheek, I said, "I don't think you're being forthcoming with why you're here."

"Oh really," he said flatly.

"No, I think the real reason you came for me is that you finally decided to test your mettle. Here you are, flirting with Medicare eligibility, with hair beginning to gray, four kids—most of them grown and out of the house—and a cute little brick ranch in the suburbs. You've been domesticated. Neutered. Housebroken. You've become the guy with the coin purse holding up the line at the grocery store while you fish around for a nickel. All these years of comfortably sitting behind a desk have left you with the burning desire for an adventure, and I presented you with the opportunity to finally exercise your rusty manhood. Well buddy, if you wanted an adventure, you've got one in spades, now. We'll be lucky if either of us make it out of here," I said, resting a hand on the side mirror of our five-ton troop carrier and leaning against it.

Kailas spat on his thumb, reached down, and wiped a scuff from the toe of his loafer. "Well you've just got all the answers, don't you, Cogar? Fine. As long as we're playing this little psychoanalyzing game, let me take a go with you. Why are you here, I wonder?"

"Nothing exciting there, Kailas," I sighed as I tapped at our truck's tire with my boot. "I came here to cover a story for the *Herald* and had an epiphany. I can do more good helping refugees and the injured than I could writing another article that no one will read. Besides, trying to report here is futile. The whole situation is a cesspool: a convoluted rat's nest of international meddling and sectarian violence. I mean, ask any one of these guys," I gestured toward the crowd of rebel soldiers milling about the trucks, "who's on their side and you'll get a different answer every time. It's a scrambled agglomeration of every wannabe jihadi, mercenary, and idealist freedom fighter from here to Algeria."

"And which one are you?" Kailas asked, flicking the collar of my camouflaged jacket with his pointer finger.

"Hey, I'm just as likely to be shot wearing a pair of slacks and press credentials as I would dressed as I am now."

He snorted. "So all this has nothing to do with you being bored? Not getting the same adrenaline rush you did when you first started reporting?"

"Nothing to do with that at all."

The convoy's trucks rattled to life, and we clambered aboard the last one in line. Kailas carefully dusted off a section of the wood bench before sitting down. If he'd had any idea how much blood and filth had soaked into that seat in the past few months, he wouldn't have bothered.

"So the six-month bender you went on when you came back from Cairo had nothing to do with your sudden departure for Syria," Kailas said. Persistent bastard.

"I wasn't on a bender," I argued. "I wrote a few articles for *Traveler* magazine during that time that I thought turned out to be pretty good. 'Travel Tips for Temerarious Tourists,' for instance. That's clever shit.

You never let me be witty with my headlines for the *Herald*. It's all 'Whimsy is for women's magazines,' or 'don't sacrifice clarity for cleverness, Cogar.' Alliteration aside, you're no fun."

"You produced three articles—for a travel magazine, no less—in six months, and managed to rack up a drunk and disorderly charge," Kailas said.

The soldiers beside us watched our dispute as though it were a tennis match, heads bobbing from person to person as we replied to one another. None of them spoke much English, but their fascination with our quarrel and our animated gesticulations was evident.

"First of all, that travel magazine pays a hell of a lot better than your dying newspaper, you cheap bastard," I said. "Second, there's no law against public intoxication in Illinois. The cops just drove me home."

"Regardless, you stopped writing serious news, turned up drunk every time I heard from you, and then disappeared into a civil war on the other side of the world for damn near a year. It sounds to me like you're incapable of functioning in a normal society. You need conflict to feel alive."

I opened my mouth to speak, but no rebuttal came to mind. I finally stammered, "That's not true. I just feel like my being back in Illinois is pointless. Like I'm just sitting around waiting to die. Here…well at least I feel like I'm doing something worthwhile."

Shukri jumped into the truck bed and sat down beside Kailas, sliding a mud-spattered medical bag between his legs.

"I see my note made it to you intact, Mr. Raahi," the medic said, extending a handshake to Kailas. "It's a pleasure to make your acquaintance."

"It was you?" I shouted. "Dammit, Shukri. Why?"

Shukri nudged his glasses further up the prominent bridge of his nose before folding his hands in his lap. "Frankly, my friend, it's well past time you go home. You don't belong here," he said. "This was never your fight, and although you fought it nobly, we need you to tell our story to the Americans. You've been here long enough to do that."

"I'm doing more good here than I would back in the States. You know that." It left my mind as an assertion, but it came out of my mouth sounding more like a question—doubtful and seeking affirmation.

"You've been invaluable, and have saved many lives. You can be content knowing that. But as your friend, trust me, it's better for you to leave here. You will be captured or killed if you stay. Each day your luck diminishes. I couldn't have your blood on my hands," he said, raising his hands before him like a surgeon who had just sterilized before an operation. "You're a rare find, Mr. Cogar. An honest and articulate man who knows our strife intimately. Be our voice."

"But I—"

"You have an obligation as a journalist," Kailas jumped in, seeing an opportunity to drive the point home now that he had someone with a similar opinion to back him up.

"Don't give me that shit," I said. "Who am I obligated to? You? My readers? No. I have one obligation, and it's to myself, to survive. Fuck journalism and all its pompous self-importance."

"I never thought I'd hear those words come out of your mouth," Kailas said soberly. "From the day I met you, you've wanted nothing more than to be a reporter. How could you have such a change in perspective?"

"Kailas, believe me when I tell you, with the things I've seen out there," I stabbed the air pointing toward the distant smoldering city, "and in every war zone from here to Baghdad, it's a miracle I haven't hung myself from my apartment balcony or ended up in a mental asylum. You know that PTSD thing that soldiers have after completing a few harrowing tours on the battlefield? Well I've been there with them for a decade. Ten years of watching men, women, and children—not just soldiers, Kailas—get gunned down, incinerated, blown to pieces, raped, and mutilated, and you can't understand why I wouldn't have the heart to just sit on the sidelines anymore?"

Kailas slapped the side of the truck with his palm, then shoved a finger in my face. "I told you when you were back in Cairo that I'd be happy to assign you something calmer stateside. You told me you didn't want something so cushy."

I bit my bottom lip hard and looked away. He didn't understand. In a way, I'd been damned to the same life as a career soldier. In the beginning, the job is everything, and it takes everything, too. Healthy, lasting relationships can't thrive when one half is gone, pursuing the danger where it lives. Some may keep a spouse or lover back home, but they do so the way one keeps a plastic Christmas tree, giving it attention for about a month out of the year. Your body gets bruised and battered, but you shake it off. You never expect for that pain to revisit you years later, but it does. You become stiff and rheumatic, as if slowly turning to stone. Then, one day, a guy like Kailas approaches and tells you to give it up. it's a young man's game, after all. You want nothing but to fight back, prove you're sharper than ever, that the adage about an old snake's venom being no less deadly is true. But you know, at least on some level, he's right. Still, when you're offered a desk job—in my case, a bunch of mundane domestic assignments—it pisses you off. So you find a way to weasel back in, get back out in the field doing what you're good at. But the job has taken its toll, and every morning when you slowly unfold from bed, counting scars and waiting for your ground-up joints to limber, you're reminded of it. Maybe they were right, but you know it's too late to change. It's poisoned your blood. It's slithered in and changed your DNA. It's the siren's call, the sweet, distant melody that whispers invitingly, guiding you softly toward the abyss.

That had been me, down to the letter. But instead of taking a contracting job the way an old soldier might have done, I'd run away to join the circus in Syria. And when I arrived, I discovered that this used-up, swaybacked one-trick pony could do more than write. I'd found where I needed to be.

"Kailas, you make it sound so easy, so black and white. I refuse to just waste away as a local beat reporter, but I can't keep going from war zone to war zone, watching terrible atrocities committed and doing nothing more than putting pen to paper to stop it, either. It doesn't work. The same shit just keeps happening. So I figured I had a choice: I could either pretend nothing but ponies and rainbows existed outside the walls of my apartment the way everyone back home does, or I could do something tangible for a change."

Softening, Kailas said, "Your work as a reporter is tangible, Cogar. It makes a big difference, even if you don't—."

"Shut up," I said abruptly, cocking my head and listening to a new, subtle sound in the distance. There are two characteristics shared by veterans, journalists, and refugees who have survived war: luck, and plenty of situational awareness. Ignoring the rumble of tanks in the distance or the sudden, unnatural quiet preceding an ambush has a way of making you dead quickly.

"You've taken a turn for the juvenile, Cogar. Shut up? What are you, fourteen?"

I hushed him. The steady, almost unnoticeable chop of helicopter rotors hung on the air. Assad's gunships were coming.

"Hinds! Get out of the trucks!" I screamed a second too late. The air filled with a sound like a giant sweeping a finger over a massive washboard. *Braap braap.* Emerging from the heavy smoke masking the skyline, a trio of camouflaged, Russian Mi-24 helicopters swept over us. Strings of 30x165mm armor-piercing rounds clawed the earth. Punctured steel. Burst through soft flesh.

I grabbed Kailas's shirtfront and dragged him over the truck bed's edge. Before my shoulder struck the ground, I spotted Shukri toppling from the truck as a round struck him squarely in the chest. The vehicle erupted in flame, so close and so hot, it ignited my sleeve. Rolling into a culvert beneath the road, Kailas and I covered our ears as the helicopters hovered and continued their relentless assault, the concussion of the rounds slapping the earth vibrating against our soles.

5
Too Much Blood on My Hands

When the echo of the final explosion died away, reverberating between distant rolling hills made bare by goats and artillery, I scrambled to the blackened ruins of the convoy, rifling through the mangled, smoldering bodies looking for Shukri.

"Shukri, where are you, man?"

A hand rose feebly from beneath a pile of corpses. I dug frantically at the farrago of charred limbs to free him. Unsure of whether the helicopters would return, I slipped my hands beneath the medic's arms and dragged him into the safety of the ditch. A crimson trail followed as I pulled him through the mud. He choked on short, ragged breaths, his glasses shattered but still hanging limply from his ears.

"Mr. Cogar, I think...I've had it."

"No, no. We'll fix you up in no time, all right? Just keep those breaths coming, buddy." I wiped the blood from my hands against my pant legs as I worked to elevate the wounded man's legs. "Kailas, find his bag. There should be an Asherman chest seal and a packet of hemostatic powder in there. I need them both. Now."

No questions, no hesitation, Kailas nodded and scrambled over the embankment in search of the medic's kit.

"Mr. Cogar...it's too late," Shukri wheezed.

"No, it's not. Save your energy, okay?"

He shook his head groggily as I held my palms tight against the wound in his chest. "Please, go back. Go to America. Promise me. Promise me," he repeated softly as he slipped away.

Kailas slid into the culvert, dragging the medic's bag.

"I found the bag, but I don't know what that chest-seal thing looks like...."

"It's too late, Kailas," I said, rocking back and wiping my eyes with my forearm.

As he stared at the corpse of the man who had only minutes before been conversing with us, I watched as Kailas experienced, for the first time in his life, mortality in all her stark ugliness. Few people see a death so abrupt as one on a battlefield. Sure, Kailas had lost his parents, both in their mid-eighties, and he'd gotten a couple heartbreaking phone calls and had to process it all and grieve and plan the funerals. But to see a living, breathing, corporeal life taken so needlessly and suddenly was another beast entirely.

It's something a person never gets used to. Witnessing human life crushed is unforgettably painful, as though someone has reached inside your chest and torn out something vital, a piece of your humanity carelessly broken off from the whole, leaving behind a jagged edge that stabs your insides periodically and never lets you forget what you've seen. Kailas raised a hand to his mouth, but there was no stopping it. Vomit spilled into the mud.

I stood and walked away, leaving Shukri's corpse resting against the muddy embankment. I wiped his blood off on my pants and began digging urgently through my pockets for another ya-dom stick; the sight and smell of the tattered bodies and the guttural heaving sound of my mentor retching had made me sick to my stomach, too.

I didn't get the inhalant into my nostril in time. The acidic bile climbed my esophagus, and I heaved up what little I'd had to eat that day.

"Shouldn't we bury the bodies?" Kailas asked a few minutes later, slowly climbing toward me as he wiped at his mouth with the back of his hand. He swallowed hard and looked at the sky, eyes shining with tears, in an attempt to keep from being sick again.

"Wouldn't bother," I said, taking a shallow breath. The earthy, putrid smell of upset dirt and fresh blood saturated the air, making it difficult to breathe without gagging. Looking at the gunmetal swirl of clouds above, I watched as a lone vulture slowly wound corkscrews above the wreckage. "Crows and wild dogs will get at them long before you're through."

"But Shukri, at least. He was your friend."

"The spirit has left the vessel, Kailas. Above the dirt or below it, it doesn't matter now. Besides, the longer we stay here, the more likely we are to be found and killed, too. We need to get to the city, find some rebels to give us a ride to the border, and get you on a plane back to Chicago."

I guided him in the direction of the city proper.

"You mean get *us* on a plane back to Chicago," Kailas corrected.

"No, I meant what I said."

"You can't stay here, Cogar," he said in a way I imagined he would speak to one of his kids who had just declared they were going to live at the zoo from then on. As though the thought of me staying in Syria was so plainly ridiculous, it became adorable in a naive way. Like I was an Alzheimer's patient sitting on a park bench, thinking it was a bus stop, determined to return home to a place that had been bulldozed decades before.

I stared angrily at the ground without speaking. I was in no mood for arguing. I'd lost a close friend, and the way things were looking, there was a very good chance I'd lose another before I could get him out of the country.

I began thinking about the border, fully aware we might not live long enough to get that far. Getting into the country had been easy enough, but sneaking back across would be a real trial. Turkish border guards were far more careful when dealing with people exiting Syria than those entering, American or otherwise. And I didn't have to stop and check the inside of my shoe for how much currency I had left; it wasn't going to be enough to bribe our way across. We'd need to find a compassionate NGO willing to lie on our behalf to get us home. And all the sane ones had cleared out of the country months before.

After a quarter mile, Kailas cleared his throat. "I'm sorry about your friend, Cogar."

Staring at the jagged city skyline, buildings lining the horizon like a mouth full of broken teeth, I sighed.

"Yeah, me too. But he knew what staying here meant."

"What's that?"

"Certain death. It's just a question of time. Spend a few days here and you'll probably be fine. Spend a few months here; you're pushing your luck. Two years like Shukri did? You're on borrowed time."

"Why would anyone stay here?" Kailas asked, more to himself than to me. "Why would you stay here, knowing this?"

I kicked a piece of gravel and watched it bounce along the shattered pavement.

"Places like this one attract a lot of evil people, Kailas. Those who enjoy killing. Those who have no regard for life. A few decent ones have to stick around to keep the balance."

Kailas stopped and planted his hands on his hips, looking around at the desolation. "I hate to break it to you, Cogar, but I think evil's winning."

****

Monrovia, Liberia
June 2003

Our rusty Toyota Hilux rolled down a crude red clay road, following a convoy of crude vehicles filled with crude men on their way to Liberia's besieged capital city—Monrovia. They were rebels, a collection of self-proclaimed warlords in t-shirts and threadbare American basketball uniforms seeking to depose Liberian President Charles Taylor. They called themselves the Liberians United for Reconciliation and Democracy. LURD. An acronym fittingly ugly for the war in which it played a key role.

Seated across from me, a ten-year-old soldier—skin the color of onyx, sleeves of his too-large uniform rolled up to expose skeletal arms—puffed his cheeks as he attempted to inflate a bubble from the stick of gum I'd given him.

"Tell him my bubble's bigger," I said from the corner of my mouth as I leaned toward my guide, a Muslim Mandinka warrior

nicknamed *DJ Cannibal*—a *nom de guerre* he'd acquired both to protect his identity and to strike fear in the hearts of his enemies.

Bubblegum spoke to me in English, but I only caught a few words.

I asked Cannibal what the kid had said. He was too distracted to respond, chewing anxiously on a fresh roll of *Khat*—a shrub that gives an amphetamine-like high—rubbing his palm up and down his thigh. He had good reason to be uneasy; Monrovia was a ragged, festering sore, oozing every toxic violation of fundamental human rights conceivable. The air was stifling, filled with mosquitoes and biting black flies. The ditches lining the roads were filled with stagnant pools of human excrement. The men fought the government, malaria, and AIDS.

"He says the gum isn't as fun as heroin," Cannibal said after additional prodding.

I laughed. He didn't.

I slipped my voice recorder from a pocket of my new vest. I'd bought the jacket as a gift to myself upon my graduation from college the year before. It was a sharp little number in British khaki, with padded shoulders, fifteen pockets, and little brass grommets for ventilation. The travel outfitter I'd purchased it from had charged a premium, but I'd seen war photographers and foreign correspondents wearing them in Iraq, and had decided that it was an essential piece of kit for any self-respecting reporter. Flipping the recorder on, I held it toward Cannibal.

"So, what's the rebel strategy once we reach Monrovia?"

"Fight and kill many men," he said plainly as he moved from the wood bench seat to straddle the back corner of the pickup truck's bed. *The experienced fighters often did this in the faint hopes that, should their vehicle roll over a landmine, they'd be thrown clear.*

Shouts came down the line from the convoy's front, trucks stopping and passengers craning their necks to see why. Abandoning his efforts to blow a bubble, Bubblegum dropped from the edge of the truck. His bare feet navigated the tire-scooped dirt as he went to investigate. Though dressed and armed like an adult, the rifle slung over his narrow shoulders and the jouncing, exultant way only a child can move gave him away.

Curiosity piqued by the interruption, Cannibal moved to stand on the truck's cab, using the KPV heavy machine gun mounted in the truck's bed to pull himself up.

"Cannibal, what exactly are the rebels fighting against?" I asked, stabbing my voice recorder toward him as he continued to move away from me.

He replied, "Taylor is a bad man. Very bad. Corrupt. We must kill him for our people. We take Monrovia, we win the war."

It seemed peculiar that a man who had been a willing participant for years in the systematic rape and murder of innocent civilians would argue that the president's absence of morality was the reason for the civil war. Neither side had any qualms about using child soldiers. Both were guilty of butchering untold thousands of civilians in their mortar strikes and exchanges of small arms fire. Seventy percent of the country's women had been raped. Some of the rebels had shown me small, dry flaps of skin they kept in their wallets—ritualistically severed labia.

I held my tongue.

Bubblegum came running back, followed by a dozen other child soldiers. In his outstretched hand, raised as if gripping a kite string, was something red. An organ. A heart.

"Cannibal, what's he doing with that?"

"Watch, Mister Cogar."

The boy climbed back into the truck, waved the bloody organ in the air where the other boys could see him, and began shouting.

"What's he saying?"

Cannibal translated the boy's poor English. "This is a general's heart. I offer it up, and eat it all to take his strength."

The boy turned and stared at me as he ate the flesh, smiling impishly as blood trickled down his chin.

I was twenty-three years old. The extent of my time abroad up to that point had been spent riding in a Humvee with American soldiers in Iraq. This was the most repulsive human behavior I'd seen—beyond the scope of anything I could have even imagined or dreamt in a nightmare—and it was a kid doing it. I puked down the front of my vest.

Everyone laughed.

The laughing continued until the boy had finished his meal. When Bubblegum turned his back, smiling as if he'd just won a medal during school track and field day, Cannibal raised his rust-pocked FAL rifle, planted the muzzle squarely between the kid's shoulder blades, and fired. The .30-caliber bullet severed Bubblegum's spine, blood pooling around our shoes as the child slumped and convulsed in the truck's bed, his blank eyes rolling into his skull, mouth open to reveal bloodstained teeth.

"The fuck did you do that for?" I screamed, my throat burning from the stomach acid that had passed through, my lips dry. I

desperately sorted through the ways in which I could most quickly get away from this godforsaken country. Gripping the splintery wooden bench under me, I tucked my feet to my chest to escape the pooling blood and began to cry.

Withdrawing a dented aluminum canteen from his pack, Cannibal unscrewed the top, grabbed the kid's corpse, and rolled it to its side to better let the blood flow from the bullet hole into the mouth of the canteen. When he'd collected enough to fill it halfway, Cannibal took a long drink and held the canteen toward me as though offering me a beer.

"The blood of the young will make you strong in battle, Mister Cogar. Drink. You will need his strength in the fight ahead."

I pinched my eyes shut and sought some pure thought to anchor myself. A math problem, a museum painting, anything to shake the picture of the viscera bursting from that kid's chest and the nonchalant expression on Cannibal's face as he offered me his canteen.

A poem. I envisioned the thumb-worn anthology of Robert W. Service poems stuffed in my desk back home. My lips sought the words, long ago memorized.

There's a race of men that don't fit in,
A race that can't stay still;
So they break the hearts of kith and kin,
And they roam the world at will.

6

The Wild War Tourist

Aleppo, Syria
June 2013

Rain fell. Drops so cold, they shot painful electrical pulses along bare skin. The city vanished behind a wall of ashen vapor.

"Typical. As if the day wasn't shitty enough before, now we get to be wet, too. That's just great," Kailas grumbled, holding his hand out as the pattering rain increased in volume, thudding into the soft soil, ricocheting off of twisted artillery and dented car hoods.

"Actually, it is," I said, pulling my coat collar tight to my neck. "You may have noticed the terrain's pretty open here—deadly conditions when Assad's helicopter and MiG pilots have a clean line of sight. A little cloud cover and rain should improve our odds for a bit."

Kailas stared at me for a moment before he spoke, his voice grave as he blinked away the rain. "I sometimes forget that you're not the same punk kid I brought home from that library all those years ago. You've learned a lot out here, haven't you?"

I swallowed hard. Kailas didn't typically bring up our introduction; he knew it was a painful part of my life I was perfectly happy relegating to the unswept repository of my memory.

The day he invited me to his home, Kailas holding the hand of his then six-year-old daughter, Page, as he addressed me, I'd already been on the run for over a week. I'd left the youth shelter again—this time for good, I'd told myself—and was spending each night sleeping on the floor of a public library bathroom. Kailas spoke to me as one adult to another, with a respect I was entirely unused to hearing. He brought me into his home, fed me, clothed me, and gave me money for a deposit on my own apartment.

He'd only asked that I pay him back for his kindness by working for the *Chicago Herald* as an intern. He'd saved my life that day, and I couldn't shake the feeling that, like the father he'd been to me, he was disappointed that I'd been at constant work to risk that life ever since.

I cleared my throat and mumbled, "Well the alternative to learning those tricks is death. I'm still here, so yeah, you could say I've picked up a few things."

We entered the city, pinballing our way through a labyrinth of shoulder-width alleyways. At each turn, I'd stop, Kailas would collide with my back, I'd curse at him under my breath, and I would slowly peek around the corner until I was sure we were safe to proceed. While I moved with caution, cognizant of where I planted each foot, eyes scanning windows above for the shuffle of a curtain or the glint of a rifle barrel, Kailas blundered along as if in a hurry to reach his bus stop.

We eventually reached one of the main thoroughfares piercing the bowels of the city. Voices and the crackle of scattered small-arms fire echoed between the buildings' bullet-pocked facades. I gestured for Kailas to hang back while I checked to make certain the troops ahead of us were rebels. Satisfied by their lack of uniforms or heavy-duty military hardware, I returned to find Kailas staring open-mouthed at our surroundings. I recognized the look on his face: bewilderment and curiosity, awe and disorientation. What had once been a bustling metropolis had been reduced to a rubble-strewn wasteland, a moonscape punctuated by dusty shadows of multi-story edifices. Entire city blocks lay in crumbled piles, like sand castles beset by a rising tide. Fire escapes, bent and missing rungs, hung at impossible angles like twisted, crooked smiles. They creaked eerily with each earth-shaking impact of distant artillery. The ground underfoot crunched with brass and steel shell casings. But the most jarring thing about it was almost no one was there. From two and a half million residents to only a few hundred thousand in just months, Aleppo looked better suited as a backdrop to a zombie film than as a city the size of Chicago.

"Cogar, don't you find yourself questioning why you're here when everyone that used to live here has run away? Why fight and bleed for a cause that even the people of Syria obviously don't believe in?"

I scoffed. "Causes. Causes are the domain of privileged, effete liberal-arts students, circling their leased Audis for a brief protest in the park before the weather gets too bad and they retreat to the organic coffee shop in the city's trendy district for a soy latte. It's just self-flagellation performed in public. Take a fucking picture and be sure your friends see it on social media so they can appreciate how worldly and caring you are. How ashamed you are to be privileged, but not so ashamed as to abandon your luxury. Causes are for the naïve and the puerile. They produce the same satisfied feeling of accomplishment that follows a roaring orgasm. But it's not sex; it's just masturbation."

I stooped and picked up an especially large artillery shell casing and handed it to him. "That'd make a cool trash can for your office." He looked it over briefly before discarding it into an empty shell crater.

"Simply put, Kailas, causes have no place here. It's all about survival. These people have been conditioned to scratch at the dirt to survive until they're forced to a new mud pit by a warlord or general or—hell—greedy neighbor with a bigger, better-armed family than theirs. They have no illusions about fixing this because they've been waist-deep in this cesspool since the day they were born. They accept death as inevitable. Life is cheap and self-preservation is the guiding rule. The only person who cares about your survival around here is you. Those not compelled by some misbegotten religious fervor do what any animal faced with extinction does. They run."

Kailas only grunted, chewing a fingernail thoughtfully as he no doubt considered what he would have done if the roles had been reversed, and he and his family were here when the fighting had begun.

"Cheer up," I said, elbowing his arm playfully. "Things could be worse. Whenever I get depressed, I just remind myself that I could be hanging from a bridge overpass in Mexico."

"At least the weather is nicer there. And it's not an active war zone," Kailas said.

"Debatable on that last part."

Kailas stopped walking, shuffling his suit jacket off and tossing it over his shoulder. Dark rings of sweat had discolored the underarms of his otherwise spotless shirt. "Don't you have a satellite phone we can use to call for help?"

Patting my pockets as if searching for a cell phone, I said, "I must have left it in my other pants."

"You could just say you don't have one instead of being a tit about it."

"Well of course I don't have one, Kailas. You don't pay enough for me to have nice things. Other reporters get satellite phones, hotels with room service, high-risk insurance coverage, people who call ahead and coordinate fixers to meet them at the border, nice cameras—"

"I loaned you one of the *Herald's* Nikon SLRs before you left for Syria," Kailas interrupted. "What happened to it?"

"Confiscated. First day," I lied, recalling the surprised look on the pawn shop owner's face when I readily agreed to his lowball offer on the camera.

Snapping his fingers and giving me an 'I told you so' look, Kailas said, "That's why I don't give you nice things. You never bring them back."

"Well you send me into places where people have really good taste, and very few scruples about stealing. Besides, I wouldn't want a sat phone here even if you had sent one with me. Assad's regime tracks sat-phone signals; he killed a couple of reporters from the *Sunday Times* with a rocket attack that way last year. I prefer Assad and his buddies never even know I'm here."

"That's so bewildering to me that anyone would intentionally kill a reporter," Kailas said. "I mean, even aside from the obvious immorality of killing someone, anyone, isn't killing a journalist against the Geneva Convention?"

"Killing a non-combatant has been officially against the rules for centuries, but I don't think Assad is too concerned about international law at this point. Times have changed. The battlefield isn't the way Rommel left it: There's no honor or mercy, chivalry or nobility left, and it's been like that for longer than I've been alive. The one saving grace for journos like me was that the bad guys used to need us. We were a conduit to people they wanted to reach. Now, with technology the way it is, extremists, dictators, gangsters, they don't need journalists to have their voices heard. They all have websites and social media profiles just like everyone else. I know a half dozen Somalian pirates who could teach the average teenage girl a thing or two about the proper technique for shooting selfies. It's like an ugly guy putting together an online-dating profile; these guys can make themselves look as good as they want now because they're the ones controlling the story. Before, they had to play the game. If they wanted people to know they existed, the only way to do it was to play ball with those passing along the message. People like me. If they treated me like shit, lied to me, endangered my life, they knew the story would come out with them looking bad. Now, journalists are just another obstacle separating the crazies from their audience. Better as kidnapping or assassination fodder. Truth has become something to disguise, to paint over. Journalists, those obnoxious harbingers of fact, just get in the way."

"How is it you write for a newspaper?" Kailas said as he stopped to watch a rebel team set up an 82mm Soviet mortar, dragging tins of ammunition toward them as they angled the tube in the direction of the distant rifle fire and scooted the bipod through the gravel to support it. "With these long-winded diatribes of yours, I would have figured you'd have taken to writing books by now."

"I can't sell most articles I write. Who the hell would want to read my book?" I gave Kailas a sharp tug, pulling him around the corner.

"Hey, what's the big idea?" he said, peeling my fingers from his shirt. "You're kind of a bully in war zones, all grabby and pushy."

"Stand back. You don't know whether those guys are using found ammunition or not."

"What difference does that make?" Kailas asked, taking a few steps back so he could continue to watch the mortar crew at work.

I explained, "Long story short, I'm not sending you home without all the limbs you brought with you. Assad's men play dirty. Whenever they capture an enemy supply shipment, they salt it with faulty or booby-trapped ammunition, and then they leave it behind. It's an old-school trick that's been used in every war since the '40s. Grenades that explode the second you pull the pin, explosive cartridges that destroy your gun and send pieces of the receiver into your face, and mortar shells," I gestured toward the mortar team as one of the men dropped a finned projectile down the tube and swept his hands over his ears in one fluid motion, "that explode the instant they're primed."

"They're so young," Kailas whispered, his brow furrowed. The mortar team was made up of four teenagers, slight of build and young in the face, all of them wearing t-shirts and cargo pants. They wouldn't have looked out of place on the bleachers at a high school football game.

I rubbed my cheek and looked away. "Everyone's a participant in the war, whether they want to be or not. The schools have been leveled, there's no work to be had, obviously, and if these kids are going to be killed by Assad as non-participants anyway, they might as well join the fight and go out swinging."

"What a terrible paradigm." Kailas stared at the kids as they worked, holding the image close until the heat seared it into his memory.

"Agreed. You should tell Assad in your best stern, fatherly voice that you disapprove of his methods."

"If we see him, I'll be sure to do that," Kailas said, picking up a car's sideview mirror from the street and using it to guide him as he fished an errant eyelash out of his eye.

A few hundred yards away, rebels fired their rifles around a 90-degree corner in the street, the gunshots echoing between the buildings. The shots were interrupted by fighters on both sides exchanging curses and dares; they were so close to one another, they could hold entire arguments during reloads.

It was like a war from a past century.

"*W ba'dein ya ghaby?*" a man asked, his voice taunting.

"*Ahana btameleen aktar al harb men ento!*" A woman's voice—higher-pitched, but equally acerbic—shot back. I glanced at each of the rebels standing nearby until I saw her. A woman with a dark complexion and the sort of elegantly hewn Mediterranid bone structure one would expect of Hera or Juno berated a male soldier, tapping his chest angrily with one hand, pinching a cigarette in the other. A rifle hung from a worn canvas strap slung over her shoulder.

In this part of the world, it was exceedingly rare to find a woman clearly standing as equal to her male counterparts, armed, and not wearing a hijab.

Kurdish. Definitely Kurdish. I recalled the frosty night I spent in the Qandil Mountains of northern Iraq, and the warm skin of a Kurdish woman soldier who shared my sleeping bag. She was a member of the Free Life Party of Kurdistan that spent most of its time pressuring Iran with guerilla attacks. She'd made it clear she was having sex with me, not the other way around. I walked with a limp for a week following, but it'd been worth it.

I caught only a few words of their argument, but the man's body language made clear that he didn't think highly of a woman carrying a gun and fighting alongside men.

"How can a country be free if its women aren't?" I asked as we approached.

The male soldier scanned me from head to toe and grunted dismissively before walking away, shaking his head.

Tossing her cigarette beneath her boot and driving it into the dirt with her heel, the young woman said in perfect English, "Thanks for the contribution, American. Just like your countrymen. All the wrong words at all the wrong times, and nothing of substance to back them up."

Feisty and clever. I immediately liked her.

"Hasty generalizations are unbecoming of a beautiful woman."

Verbally stumbling, taken aback by my compliment, she replied, "Another crazy from America. Just some privileged, would-be jihadist fighting for a cause you don't understand." Standing before me and staring into my eyes coldly, she continued, "So what, you make some friends on the Internet who convinced you to come fight for Allah? Come to collect your virgins?"

Imagining what she looked like without her fatigues on, I said, "Naw, I wasn't a huge fan of the retirement package Allah was offering. Besides, virgins aren't my thing. I prefer a woman who can teach me a thing or two."

She spat at my feet. Immune to my charms, apparently.

"Your kind undermine our efforts, and keep those who would help us succeed from committing to our cause for fear of being allied with terrorists. We'd be better without you."

I understood her frustration. Moderate freedom fighters like this young woman, the first to pick up arms against Assad, had been slowly replaced by better-funded religious extremists with an agenda completely apart from restoring peace to the country.

That said, she had me all wrong.

I stepped toward her, my movements slow, deliberate. She countered my approach boldly, stopped, cocking a hip and crossing her arms. Her eyes smoldered with an unflinching intensity. There were those in life who talked a big game about things they had seen and done, and there were those who didn't need to say a word. Confidence like hers didn't stem from arrogance, it had been earned the hard way, ground to a fine point by things that would only swim to the surface for breath during nightmares and flashbacks.

I leaned in, my lips an inch from her ear, and whispered, "I don't think you have any idea why I'm here. That bothers you, doesn't it? I'm not a jihadist or journalist, and I don't work for an NGO or the CIA. So what does that make me?"

A bright flash blinded us both, the young woman scrambling to shoulder her rifle. For a moment, I thought I'd been in the proximity of an exploding artillery round. I touched my face, feeling for blood, worried I might find essential parts missing.

As my vision cleared, I did a double take. An Asian man wearing a boonie hat grinned and raised his camera—a pricey Leica S2 with an obtrusive telescopic lens the size of a human arm and an external flash that had somehow channeled the power of the sun.

"Good photo!" he cheered before turning and jogging toward the gunfire down the street.

"It's like a fucking zoo here," Kailas said, incredulous as he stepped beside me. "I thought I'd seen it all, but the kind of bizarre bullshit that seems to happen here every five minutes makes Chicago look like a private-school playground."

"Wars have a rude way of upsetting normalcy," I mumbled, eyes following the man as he skittered across the street through enemy fire, shooting photos and narrating the experience to the wearable video camera he'd strapped to his chest. "But that one's a first for me, too." I'd never actually seen a war tourist during my time on the battlefield; they always seemed to end up captured or killed before I could observe them in their natural habitat. He'd raced through our lives with the same frivolity of a chubby neighbor kid passing through a drunken backyard barbecue, leaving everyone confused and curiously ashamed.

Turning back to the Kurdish soldier, I asked, "Can I speak with you in private for a moment?"

She looked at me doubtfully, but must have resolved that I was harmless. With a nod, she gestured for me to follow her toward a stack of pallets in an adjacent alleyway.

I lowered my voice as I sat down, careful to keep Kailas from overhearing me. "My friend, the Indian fella? He just got into the country, and I need to get him back out. Do you know of anyone who's heading for the border today?"

"So your friend doesn't share your love for war?"

"Why are you saying that? Again, you know nothing about me. Do you see me carrying a gun? I'm here to help you."

"You're not much help to anyone without a gun." She sighed. Looking over her shoulder, she tapped her foot anxiously, "I know of a convoy heading north tomorrow morning. But they're half a kilometer west of here at least. I can't spare any fighters to take you there, and to be honest, I can't be sure if they've moved to a different location. I think you'd be better off going back the way you came."

"I'd prefer to take my chances in the city," I said, rubbing the dust from my eyes. "Assad's Hinds are out in force today. They killed everyone in the unit I was with this morning."

She shook her head incredulously. "I still don't understand. Why are you here?"

"I got off on the wrong stop and they keep delaying my flights," I joked. "How about you, is this your tabor? You're with the YPJ, right?" I asked, gesturing toward the others.

She nodded, but swallowed hard, her eyes taking on a glassy, far-off look. She swept the frayed end of her shemagh against her cheek like a child clutching a security blanket. My eyes settled on her cheeks— smooth, but covered in a fine composite of sweat and dust. This country did that; it distressed all the soft, beautiful things, leaving them tarnished. "I was a schoolteacher once. It seems so long ago, now. An artillery shell destroyed my classroom when I was at home, sick. The few students that survived are refugees, now. Assad owes me blood for the lives he took, and that's a debt I intend to collect on, even if it costs me my life."

"I hope it doesn't."

She smirked and wrapped a hand around my shoulder gently.

"Be careful, American. Move quickly, and watch your corners. If at all possible, stay off the streets and move building to building. Assad's men don't care if you're carrying a gun or not, so I suggest you get one at first opportunity. There's no shortage of them around."

I smiled the way one would if asked by their sweet old grandmother when they were going to get married and settle down. To her, no doubt, it was a perfectly legitimate suggestion. Why wasn't I carrying a gun? This was a war zone after all, and guns were as crucial to its existence as air to a living thing. It wasn't as though I hadn't been asked about this before, or that it even demanded an uncomfortable explanation. It was that the answer seemed so plainly obvious to me that I couldn't bring myself to dispute the point. Asking me why I didn't have a gun was like asking someone at a wake why they aren't eating. After all, there are plenty of forks around.

I didn't come here for the food, thanks.

"What's the best way out of here?" I asked.

"You can either go back the way you came half a kilometer, or you can follow that photographer through the gunfire, across the street. Assad's forces are tightening the noose around us."

"Thanks. And good luck. If this war ever ends, and you get a free minute, shoot me a message, will you?" I asked, slipping a wrinkled business card from my pocket and pressing it into her hand. "If you feel like having a cup of coffee with a crazy American."

"I'll keep you in mind," she said. Looking at the business card, she smirked and yelled to me as I walked away, "I thought you said you weren't a journalist."

"I'm trying to quit."

7
The Round That Gets You

Rejoining Kailas, I rolled my shoulders and took a deep breath. He wasn't going to like what I had to say—I didn't want to say it at all—but these were the sorts of decisions I had to make all the time. Shitty choice one or two?

"You feeling athletic today, old man?" I asked, nudging him.

"You arrogant prick, I'm in better shape than you are." Kailas snorted, rolling his shirtsleeves at the elbow. "All those years you've spent drinking and smoking and staying out until the early hours of the morning, I was eating salads and getting my eight hours each night."

"Good, good. Because where we're going, you're going to need to be in prime shape."

The defiant hardness faded from Kailas's features. "Why? Where are we going?"

I pointed down the street just as one of the rebels scrambled into cover, firing wildly over his shoulder as incoming fire chiseled away bits of brick from the building's façade overhead.

"Oh, no. Why? Can't we go around?" Kailas asked.

"There is no around. There's only through," I said, stooping to tighten the laces on my boots. "Come on. It'll make a good story to tell your kids."

"If I live to see them again."

"Oh come on. You're far more likely to be killed by an artillery strike than by small-arms fire. Most of those guys can't shoot for shit, anyway." A mortar thumped nearby, followed by a distant rumble.

Kailas turned his head slowly. The look he gave me said very explicitly, "You're not selling me on this."

I continued, trying hard to sound reassuring. "We just need to get across that street, and we'll be free and clear. It'll be smooth sailing from there, okay? Just, whatever you do, don't stop running until you reach the other side. Look at it like playing tag. With bullets."

"You're being pretty nonchalant about gambling with our lives," Kailas said, dragging his fingernails against his scalp.

"Gambling only becomes a problem if you make a habit of losing."

Stopping at the edge of the intersection beside two rebel gunmen in jeans and hooded sweatshirts, I looked over at my mentor as he dropped to his knees, covering his head.

"Would you stop ducking every time there's a gunshot? Please? You're embarrassing me."

"Sorry for trying to safeguard my life, Cogar," Kailas said, flinching visibly as another slug slapped harmlessly against a concrete abutment 20 feet overhead.

"You're not safeguarding anything. You'll never even hear the round that gets you." Chewing a splinter from the pad of my thumb as I peeked out from cover, I continued. "Bullets travel faster than sound. You're ducking every time you hear a gunshot, but that bullet has already passed you. You may actually find it liberating to not have to worry about it anymore." Another round zipped by an inch above my right ear, and I recoiled, ducking further into cover. "Okay, that one was worrisome."

A burning car in the middle of the street coughed a dark, steady flow of smoke into the air. Somewhere close by, the urgent shouts of a group of men was followed by a thunderous detonation.

"You ready?" I asked.

"Fine," Kailas said. "But you go first."

"No, you'll want to go first."

"Oh sure, send me as bait," he said. I spotted the slightest tremble in his hands as he re-tied his shoes.

"They aren't expecting anyone to run across, so you should make it with no trouble. I'm going to have a much more difficult time," I explained. "If you're lucky, they might even hit me. You're welcome. Call it an early Christmas present."

"Early? Never in your life have you thought to get me a Christmas gift."

"I was under the impression someone as miserly as yourself didn't celebrate holidays," I said.

Kailas sneered, mouth open in a false laugh. A burst of automatic rifle fire sobered him. Shuffling his feet, he said, "I don't want to go first."

"Fine. Let's settle this like old times. You call it. Odds or evens?"

"Odds."

We both threw a hand out, Kailas's with only his pointer finger extended, me with all five fingers outstretched.

I hooted and punched his arm. "Evens. You go first, just like I said."

Kailas grumbled, straightened his shirt, and stared at the alley he had to cross. He didn't need to articulate his doubt or his sudden regret for coming to Syria. The grinding of his teeth and the anxious creases in his forehead said it all. He paced for a moment, then turned and asked, "Are you sure this is a good idea, Cogar?"

"Of course not. But this is war. You do the best you can with what you've got. Go on, I'll meet you over there. Promise."

Looking at me skeptically, he slowly dropped into a track runner's stance. Exhaling audibly, he glanced at me once more, cursed my name, and sprinted for the opposite side of the street. The enemy fire picked up instantly.

He made it less than halfway across before catching a toe of his loafer on the jagged edge of a concrete slab. As he toppled behind the burning car, Assad's men redoubled their rate of fire, dumping ammunition at Kailas as he huddled behind the vehicle's engine block and the crumbled stone piled against it.

"I'm gonna need that," I said, snatching an SKS rifle from a teenage rebel's hands and dashing out into the street. Sliding in beside my mentor as rifle rounds snapped overhead, I laughed, "Kailas! Didn't expect to find you here. Frequent this place often?"

"Fuck, Cogar, fuck!" was all he could get out as bullets clanged through the car's body, whining as they glanced off of stones and steel.

"Ready to try it again? Run for it!" I shouted, rolling from my hiding place and firing from the hip as I dashed back toward the rebel position. With the enemy fire on me, Kailas scampered from behind the car and made it to the opposite side of the street unharmed.

Handing the stolen rifle back to its awestruck owner, I nodded my thanks, pinched my nose and sniffed deeply; then, I reentered the street.

Shallow breaths. Long strides. I blinked away tears, eyes watering as I leapt through the cloud of acrid smoke belched from beneath the incinerated car's hood. A bullet struck the tip of my boot and I stumbled.

Chest to the ground.

Pain pulsed from my knee where it had struck a rock.

I scrambled to my feet. Automatic rifle fire spat powdered concrete and gravel at my legs as the rounds burrowed into the earth. Diving for safety, I felt a hot wind pass by as Assad's men emptied the last of their magazines in my direction. They had to have been frustrated by this contemptibly brazen American running back and forth before their muzzles and escaping without a scratch.

Panting as I fingered a graze in the fabric of my pant leg, I leaned against Kailas. The poor guy mumbled a prayer, eyes pinched shut and forehead against the brick wall.

I slapped his back.

"See? Nothing to it."

8
Godforsaken Wasteland

As we climbed up a crumbled stack of shattered concrete leading to the second floor of a derelict warehouse, Kailas asked, "I've been wondering, how'd you get into the country? This is all new to me. I had to follow a bunch of other reporters in. The guide running the show charged me a thousand bucks just to tag along. Worse, he ran away and left me to get captured the minute the Syrian Army showed up. I wouldn't have paid him so much if I'd known how worthless a guide he was."

"You shouldn't have paid that much even if your guide was Marco Polo. Face it; you got taken, buddy. Someone should have taught you that the world of foreign correspondence is like one big Egyptian bazaar—you're expected to haggle."

"Like I said, this is new to me. And don't worry, I have every intention of taking that out of your next paycheck," he said, slipping as the stones beneath his hands and feet gave way. He slid a few feet down the rocky gradient and I passed him. "How'd you get here, then, oh wise one?" he shouted after me.

An exposed piece of rusty rebar caught my pant leg. I cursed and reached to extricate myself with my free hand. "Well, the Bab al Hawa gate seemed a little busy for my tastes. Too many guards, checkpoints, places for me to lose what little money I had or end up behind bars. So I ducked some barbed wire farther down the border and caught a ride with some rebels to the outskirts of Manbij. I spent a few days there before setting out with a rebel contingent." I dragged a shirtsleeve across my forehead to clear the dust and sweat. The air was dry, desert-hot and smoke-laden. "I met Shukri when I got sick; he took care of me when the others wanted to leave me behind. After that, I decided I'd help him out as a combat medic for a while. Better than floundering alone in this godforsaken wasteland."

"You were sick?"

I kicked a brick down the hill, watching it flip end over end until it shattered on the concrete below. "Very."

"Strange," Kailas said, his tongue pinned to the inside of his cheek as he scrambled up alongside me.

I tossed a pebble at him. "Even loading up on the most potent antibiotics and anti-malarial medications known to the Western world before each trip doesn't mean I'm not still a walking cesspool of foreign contagions." I made room for him, shifting my weight to a large slab of concrete. It was an excellent vantage point to take in the city, but it was exposed. I kept an eye out for movement, hoping that, if a sniper did have me in his crosshairs, he was a good enough shot to end it quickly. "."

"Still, I don't buy it," Kailas said.

"Why?"

"Because you have always, for as long as I've known you, had an impossibly ironclad constitution. Back when you were full-time at the *Herald*, you were the only one of my employees who never took a single sick day. The women and booze somehow seem to fuel your immune system."

I crawled the rest of the way inside the building and offered Kailas a hand. "I still get sick. I just don't let it stop me from doing my job."

"But this time was different?" Kailas asked. He covered his mouth and suppressed a sneeze as he passed through a cloud of dust I'd created in my ascent.

Licking my sun-chapped lips, I peeked down a long hallway—lined on both sides with rust-covered I-beams, but otherwise empty.

"You could say that."

The truth was, in the weeks it took me to get into the country and begin reporting, I'd been entirely bereft of coffee and booze, a privation my body did not appreciate. When I was younger, I could go from week-long benders to months spent living like a Buddhist monk isolated in the Tibetan mountains—not a drop of liquor or coffee nor a whiff of tobacco—and soldier on without trouble.

But times had changed.

After spending a couple of days crippled by headaches and cramps, curled into a sweating, shivering ball of wretchedness on a narrow army cot that reeked of mothballs and urine, I slowly convalesced. Shukri looked out for me during that time. He knew exactly what was happening, but he never said a word about it. Never asked, never criticized.

Seeing that I wanted to change the subject, Kailas asked, "You run into anyone from back home while you've been here? I mean, the circle of reporters that go into these places can't be that large. You must come across familiar faces now and again."

I shrugged. "I bumped into a few professional acquaintances along the northern border. They didn't recognize me in my current state, obviously." I swept a hand from my beard to my pants as if to showcase my slovenly appearance. "And they would never dream of going where we are now. Most of them just hook up with fixers in Kilis, hop into the country for the day, snap a few photos of the wounded and a burning building or two, grab a sound byte of artillery in the distance, and duck out before nightfall. They're back in a warm bed with a Turkish hooker before midnight. If I wasn't saving all my money for that penis-reduction surgery I so desperately need, I'd probably do the same thing."

Kailas didn't even smirk at my joke. He stopped and leaned against the wall, breathing heavily, sweat beading on his brow. The air inside the bombed-out building was sweltering, but it was the lingering scent of pigeon shit that had me seriously considering taking our chances with the snipers outside instead of going any farther.

"Cogar, serious question," he said, voice solemn.

"You know I don't like those. They make my voice crack and my hands sweaty."

"Well this one's been nagging at me since I got here, and I feel like I have to ask. You've been helping the rebels all this time you've been away, yeah?"

"You observant fella, you."

"Well, I may not be an international relations expert, but I have read a thing or two about the guys you're fighting alongside. Correct me if I'm wrong, but aren't they with the Muslim Brotherhood, the same guys who wanted to kill you in Egypt, and with al-Qaeda, the same guys who tried to kill you in Afghanistan?"

I scratched the bridge of my nose and reluctantly said, "Some of them are, yes."

"So you've knowingly allied yourself with known terrorists and enemies to our country. People fundamentally opposed to our very way of life. Remind me again why you're so committed to staying here."

What had started out as a legitimate question had concluded with a blatantly hostile admonition. He was playing an angle, just trying to convince me to leave with him, I knew, but his approach lacked subtlety and felt like a thumb in my eye.

I stared at him, dumbfounded for a moment, before launching into a tirade.

"You splenetic, unwashed testicle—you think I chose to fight alongside some of the most barbaric, benighted people in the modern world? You try choking down a meal as you listen to them vomit their medieval doctrine about Allah's will, giggling like fucking sorority sisters about that time they used children for human shields, or hurled acid in the face of a young woman on her way to school, or their countless sadistic conquests in their sustained sexual warfare against anyone that doesn't subscribe to their brand of crazy."

Kailas tried to calm me down. "Look, that's not what I meant, Cogar—"

I stabbed a finger in his face. "Oh no, you listen. You sit there and let me upbraid your office-chair-molded ass for lacking the moral fiber to distinguish your friends from your enemies and tell me how that feels. You blunt instrument. Of course I have a problem with being on their side, just like a renter in a slum has a problem with being surrounded by cockroaches. But here's the part you don't get: It doesn't matter that you don't like them, because the roaches find you. They smell the carrion, the shit, and they flock to it. Just because you can't get rid of them doesn't mean you're complicit in their revolting ways."

Kailas stared at me for a moment before muttering, "I feel as though you're holding something back, Cogar. You should be more forthcoming with how you genuinely feel instead of sugar-coating everything to protect my feelings."

I breathed heavily, my cheeks red as I looked down, a little ashamed of my outburst. "It's kind of a sore subject."

"I couldn't tell."

I've never been so pretentious or histrionic as to have my own "warrior code," for one, because I don't consider myself a warrior. And two, because I've never seen a man so steadfast in virtue that his code couldn't be bent or bypassed when the moment afforded the opportunity. That said, even though every moral code is fringed with gray area, the nucleus—the bloody heart of the bastard, regardless of how small it may be—is a deep, dark black. Because even a wretch like me has one or two rules that remain as unshakable as iron no matter how tempting offers of money, sex, or power may be.

I'd never been an exemplar of morality, and debauchery was one of only a few words consistently used to describe me that was polite enough to be spoken in mixed company, but the black core of my moral code was very much intact, and murder was at its center. I'd had plenty of opportunity over the years I'd spent in war zones to partake in the violence, to throw down my voice recorder and pick up a rifle, but any such thoughts, even when there was good reason for me to stand and fight alongside those I was embedded with, bounced away like arrows against the stone walls of my sacred citadel. I didn't want anyone, especially Kailas, to think I'd thrown in with the jihadists. Whatever code they followed—if they had one at all—that little black nucleus of untouchable virtue, was dim and the size of a pinprick. Kailas had asked a legitimate question, but it came off as an insinuation that I was as morally corrupt as they were. Not morally bankrupt, but the sort of twisted that was required to believe that one is virtuous and the rest of the world immoral.

As we approached a stair landing leading to the next floor, I stopped abruptly. The hairs on the back of my neck had suddenly taken to standing upright. A single bead of ice-cold sweat ran down my spine.

"What? What is it Cogar?" Kailas whispered as if speaking to a hunting dog on point. He navigated around a hole in the floor to stand by my side.

I couldn't say exactly what I was feeing at that moment, but it was as though a sudden wave of paranoia had struck me, and I wanted to run away from that building as quickly as my legs could carry me.

"I don't know. Something feels…off," I whispered.

A strange voice echoed along the empty corridor. "If you move, you die."

9
Scottish Sam

I couldn't place the accent. It was unlike anything I'd heard: English spoken with an Egyptian or Libyan undercurrent, trailed by hints of an Irish or Cockney inflection. Bizarre and chilling in its confidence.

"We're not armed," I said cautiously.

"Foolish of you to be here, then." A man in military fatigues emerged from the shadows, a pair of aviator sunglasses propped on his shaven head and a scoped Dragunov rifle pointed squarely at my chest. "Had I been with the government forces, you'd be dead right now."

"How'd you know we aren't with Assad?" Kailas asked.

"What kind of Assad loyalist would go into Aleppo without a gun? Only misguided aid workers, civilians, and journalists would think to do something so stupid. So which are you?"

"The latter," I replied, offering my hand. "Grant Cogar, *Chicago Herald*."

Kailas only nodded and pointed a thumb at me. "I'm with him."

"I'm Housam." He lowered his rifle and shook my hand. "You're a journalist? Have you read my book, *Summer Soldier*, by chance?" The man's demeanor shifted to one both eager and a bit nervous.

"Pardon?" For a moment, I thought I'd misunderstood him. A book? I stifled a chuckle as I envisioned this fierce-looking militant sniper scribbling erotic romance novels while hiding amongst the ruins of a demolished building. "I'm afraid I'm not familiar with it."

Housam took on a frustrated expression, his lips pulled into a frown. "Well, I hope you'll give it a look when you get back to Chicago. It's the first of my memoirs, written about my time with the rebels in Libya. I'm pretty sure another American journalist already wrote an article about me. You may have heard of me by a different name." He puffed up. "They call me Scottish Sam."

Scottish. His accent was Scottish.

"Of course I've heard of you!" I said, reaching for his hand and shaking it with renewed fervor. "I didn't recognize you. Wow, this is a rare treat."

I'd never heard of him. He was one of thousands of such fighters that, upon the conclusion of the Libyan Civil War, had followed the crowd to the next party up the street. But flattery would get you far in war zones, disingenuous as it might be. Ingratiating yourself with someone who holds your life in their hands can dramatically improve your comfort while in their care and your likelihood of survival. Soldiers on border-patrol duty, government officials, and policemen are all great candidates. Jihadists, on the other hand, will just thank you for the kind words, "Very kind of you to say, infidel dog," and kill you anyway.

Fortunately, most people are so eager to have their egos stroked, they seldom think to ask probing questions about whether you have, in fact, heard of them.

"Where are you two off to?" he asked.

"Trying to get away from the fighting," Kailas said, still looking at Sam with a distrustful eye.

Sam grimaced as he propped his rifle against the wall. "Well you're going the wrong direction for that," he said, slipping a cigarette and a small battery from his chest pocket. Smoothing the tape that held a short length of wire to the battery, he moved the opposite end of the wire to the battery's other end, creating a circuit. Placing the tip of his cigarette against an exposed section of the wire—glowing white—he was soon puffing away. He methodically disassembled the contraption and returned it to his pocket. "As far as you getting away from the fighting—"

"Let me guess," I said, "We should go back the way we came?"

He nodded, tapping off the glowing ash from the tip of his cigarette with his ring finger. "Wouldn't be such a bad idea. The fighting here has been steady for weeks. I doubt it will let up enough for you two to sneak through the lines." He slowly moved the cigarette back to his mouth, but let it dangle without drawing air through it. He smoked like a French woman—as if trying to tease the fumes from the cigarette. Leisurely. Bored. Nothing like the desperate draw of the needy addict. Moments of peace, the reprieve most soldiers sought during wartime to take a restful breath, Sam seemed to grudgingly accept as a tedious inevitability he just had to suffer through until the bullets started flying again.

As though he'd suddenly remembered something, Sam jogged up the stairs and returned a moment later with two plate carriers. "Here. Protective vests if you guys want them. I pulled them off the last squad of Assad's men that came through. Killed three of them in an hour. They're like lemmings, you know? Marching into the open, one after another." Sam stomped his feet, marching exaggeratedly to an imaginary military cadence, saluting to his right and left. He let out a disdainful cackle at his pantomime before returning to his cigarette.

Kailas nodded his thanks as he reached for the body armor and began adjusting it to fit his stocky form.

I shook my head, "I'll pass. I don't do body armor, especially the stuff that's still warm from the last guy it failed to protect."

Kailas stopped and looked at me apprehensively, then scanned his vest, fingering a dime-sized hole in the fabric. He gave the hook-and-loop straps a tug and let the armor fall to the floor.

"Eh, you're probably right. It's just cheap South American-made shit, anyway," Sam said coolly, stepping onto the building's exterior catwalk, eyes scanning the ground for signs of enemy troops as he stubbed out his cigarette on the balustrade. "Come on, I've got some people you might want to meet. You two hungry?"

"Famished."

We followed him as he leapt across a gaping six-foot-wide hole in the floor—one where a misstep or weak jump would mean falling several stories into the bottom of an artillery shell crater—and down a staircase that had cracked and shifted with the building.

Peeking out of the open doorway, Sam scanned for the enemy. He stood there for several minutes. Still. Unblinking. Waiting. Movement in a war zone is polarizing—there are times it can save your life, and times when it can abruptly end it. Survivors are those who know the difference.

When he'd decided it was clear, he quietly stepped out, rifle tight to his side, staying concealed in the building's shadows.

Kailas, gripping his belt in one hand and using his other to re-tuck his shirt, promptly tripped—sending a round object skittering forward along the pavement. As it rolled to a stop at Sam's feet, I realized what it was: a human skull.

And that's when I noticed them. Bones. Human bones, picked clean by rats and wild dogs, littered the street. Gutters filled to the top with the ivory-yellow masses.

Sam stopped and picked up the skull at his feet. "Assad's men, they're Neanderthals. Look at the size of this skull—couldn't fit much of a brain in there, could you?"

"These are all Assad's men?"

"Don't let the number fool you. There are many bones in the body, Mr. Cogar," Sam said, balancing the skull on his palm as if preparing to recite a line from Hamlet. "These are only a few of Assad's dogs that happened to visit the wrong neighborhood at the wrong time. I had to put the bodies somewhere where they wouldn't give my position away or warn others of my presence."

"How can you be so nonchalant about killing?" Kailas asked. He refused to look down at the piles of bones, fixing his stare instead on a tattered line of abandoned laundry on a rooftop nearby, flagging weakly in the breeze.

"If I were killing men, it would be different," Sam replied indifferently, punting the skull, the brittle bones shattering like a porcelain bowl with the impact, showering the street. "But these are vermin. There is no negotiating with a snake."

Kailas stared at him, his expression loathsome. He didn't understand how anyone could be so undisturbed by death or killing. I wanted to explain to him that a prolonged proximity to death flagellates you on a cellular level until the callouses and the scars become so thick, the pain barely registers. Sam had long ago accepted the nature of his calling, and now, what most would consider a crucial facet of fundamental human empathy had become as alien to him as killing was to Kailas.

Sam turned and resumed walking. Over his shoulder, he said, "Someone mentioned to me that your president won a Nobel Peace Prize. But what has he done for peace? Sat on his hands, perhaps. I suppose for you Americans, that's as peaceful as you get. But look at me." He shook his rifle and slapped a palm against the wood furniture. "I'm out here doing humanitarian work, giving my blood and sweat to liberate the people of Syria from that godless pig, Assad. I think I've got a good shot at winning next year's prize, don't you?"

We crawled through a culvert beneath the street. Sam splashed rainwater at a pair of cat-sized rats, scaring them out of our way as his rifle's butt stock dragged on the concrete.

Emerging on the other side, I caught just a glimpse of the shell-pocked dome of a mosque overhead before we entered into a dimly lit basement, thick with cigarette smoke and with ceilings so low, I instantly felt a pinch of claustrophobia.

"Sam here. Coming inside," Sam announced as we entered. Half a dozen men crowded around a small television, cigarettes ablaze. A black cat, missing a ragged patch of fur from its hind leg, meowed loudly as it jumped from the floor to the backrest of a threadbare plaid couch. A gas generator puttered loudly from the next room. Carelessly stacked piles of antiques and household goods, probably looted, ran the length of the walls.

"Ooh, this one's a classic," I said, pointing toward the washed-out TV screen. "Steven Seagal, *Fire Down Below*." No one turned to acknowledge us until I grabbed the cat from the couch, held its belly against the top of my head to mimic Seagal's signature black ponytail, and mirrored the actor's soft, thoughtful tone as I said, "If your daddy knew exactly how stupid you were, he'd trade you in for a pet monkey."

The room erupted with laughs. One of the men stood and nodded toward us as he flicked the butt of his cigarette into the shadows. "Coffee?"

Kailas nodded eagerly.

I declined. Even after months without, I still struggled to suppress my automatic reaction to accept offers of coffee, booze, and cigarettes. "I'm going to pass. I'm trying to kick the stuff." Rummaging through my pocket until I found one of the sticks of ya-dom, I shoved it up my nose.

"*El Amrikan...majnooneen!*" They laughed again. Crazy Americans.

"These guys are hungry," Sam said, throwing a thumb over his shoulder as he plucked a cigarette from the mouth of one of the movie-watchers, took a drag, and handed it back.

One of the men leaned over the couch and shouted as if surprised, "Alhamdulillah, your State Department sent all these. But wait," Rummaging through a pile of plastic-wrapped MRE field rations exaggeratedly, he exclaimed, "Why, it seems they've forgotten the weapons!"

More laughs. Less authentic. A joke too real to be funny.

I cleared my throat and asked, "So I take it you gentlemen are from the FSA? Everyone else around here seems to be a little more trigger-happy when it comes to foreigners."

"Not just with foreigners," Sam corrected, discovering a pack of cigarettes balancing on the arm of the couch and looking around at his friends for a light. "It's only a matter of time before Nusra, ISIS, and their ilk are fighting and killing us, too. If you don't accept their doctrine, it doesn't matter that you're fighting a common enemy. We're all dogs in the same cage, and in the end, there can be only one."

"Most of us aren't fighters, really," one of the men said in reply to my initial question. In his mid-twenties, with boyish features and an unfortunate mole the size of a grape just below his right eye, he had an unusually soft and high-pitched voice. "If we get a shot at one of Assad's soldiers, we take it, but we're not looking for a fight."

"Why are you here, then?" Kailas asked as though the young man's statement was the most idiotic he'd heard since entering the country. I needed to work with him on dialing back the vitriol. It was just part of his character, I knew, but it also wasn't going to make us any friends.

"Well, I'm a singer," the young man replied, scraping a toe of his shoe on the concrete floor, hands buried deep in his pockets. The others in the room agreed loudly.

"He's the voice of the opposition! Surely you've heard him on the radio," one of the men said enthusiastically.

I didn't have the heart to inform them that I didn't have a radio. Or a change of clothes.

"What about the rest of you? I somehow doubt you're working as a barbershop quartet," I joked.

They became silent, looking to one another doubtfully.

"Oh. I see," I said. They were smugglers. Vultures and thieves, making money off the war. It would be best to change the subject. I looked at Kailas and gave him my best 'let it go' glare.

"Would you like to see their homemade rockets?" Sam asked, trying to defuse the tension.

Showing us into another room, bare except for an industrial welder, a stack of sheet metal piled against a wall, and bags of nitrate fertilizer, the sniper pointed at a crudely constructed rocket.

"Impressive. But still, no good against aircraft," I said, running my finger along the hasty welds and rough, torch-cut triangular stabilizers. Stalagmites of welding slag crunched underfoot.

"Why does that matter?" Kailas asked. "You could still do some major damage with this."

I chewed the inside of my cheek as I made eye contact with Sam. Kailas trying to weigh in on military ordnance was like a ten-year-old trying to talk drinking stories with college students.

"These guys could win the war if it were a fair fight," I said. "Assad's airpower is his largest advantage. The FSA doesn't have much, if anything, to fight back against the helicopters and jets."

"You gave Stingers to the mujahideen in Afghanistan to fight the Russians, yet now, when the Russians are backing Assad, and those same missiles could help us bring down his gunships, you send us food," Sam said, angrily slapping an open palm against the rocket's metal side. The clang made Kailas jump.

Sam's biggest mistake was in thinking that the U.S. was interested in seeing the rebels win the war. The suits in the State Department knew perfectly well that the rebels couldn't win without a substantial, and costly, military intervention. Instead, they did what they knew how to do so well: They discreetly backed the rebels with only enough guns and supplies to keep the war going. The longer the fighting continued, the longer Hezbollah, Iran, and Russia would bleed. The FSA couldn't win, but the Americans didn't want to give an easy victory to Assad and his backers, either. It was cold. It was businesslike. But most of all, it was a risky, shortsighted strategy sure to end in some fresh new disaster we'd all end up paying for later.

What the policymakers in Washington and the Western intelligence agencies didn't realize was that their lukewarm support was driving the few moderate rebels into the waiting arms of the jihadists. The jihadists didn't have funding problems. They had a blank check from the wealthy Gulf-State Arabs. They had guns. They had a chance of winning. They were batshit crazy, but who wasn't around here? If things continued the way they had been, the FSA would cease to be a viable fighting force, leaving behind only Assad and the hordes of Sunni militants to duke it out for control. And if it came right down to who we wanted in power the least, it would be a legitimate coin toss between those stone-age jihadist motherfuckers and an Iranian lapdog named Bashar.

"You say 'you' as though I'm the one doing it personally. I'm not. Promise." I chuckled, holding my hands up submissively.

Sam nodded and sighed. "I'm sorry. It's just frustrating. You're absolutely right; we could win this war with the right equipment. We've got the heart, we just haven't got the ordnance."

We all looked to our feet.

"Where did you say you worked, Mr. Cogar?" Sam asked suddenly, raising an eyebrow.

"The *Chicago Herald*."

"Ha!" Leaning over, he picked up a newspaper from the floor, shook the dirt from it, folded it, and handed it to me. "What are the odds?"

I laughed as I accepted the paper, running my finger along the familiar flag. "No kidding. Why'd you have this?"

"The cat box," he replied sheepishly, gesturing beneath the rocket. "We don't have litter, so we use newspaper."

I looked at Kailas smugly. Just like I've always said: Aside from the funny pages, our paper could be blank. People only used it to wrap gifts and line pet cages.

"The imagery of cat shit on paper reminds me," Kailas said as I scanned the paper looking for a date. "You've got a stack of reader mail waiting for you back home, Cogar."

"Anything that looked promising?"

"Mostly the usual suspects from what I saw at a glance. Readers angry at you for injecting political bias in your work, some angry because you're not political enough, a few trying to save your eternal soul, and one prison inmate who wants to marry you."

"Is she cute? And is she in for a violent crime? That's a deal breaker," I said, folding the newspaper and sliding it into my pocket to read later.

"It's a he. And he's a serial rapist."

We ate lunch. Kailas half-heartedly picked through a freeze-dried square of vegetarian lasagna. He'd carefully selected it from the pile of MREs for its lower calorie count. Culinary suicide.

Sam parked himself at a desk in the corner and began handloading rifle rounds. The kid with the mole sang softly and strummed a stolen guitar that was missing a string. He had an unpolished machine-gun vibrato I found distracting. I waited until Sam had finished meticulously weighing the powder for another round before I pulled him aside.

"Is there any chance you'd know a quick way to get us out of the country?"

He laughed at first, thinking I was making a joke. Then, he cleared his throat and suddenly became very interested in the callouses on his hands. "I don't know what to tell you, Mr. Cogar. The country is fragmented, making travel very difficult and dangerous. It's bad enough that you can't predict where Assad's MiGs or Hinds will be, but every day our men shift ground, too; what was controlled by Assad yesterday may be ours today, and vice versa. I'm not even comfortable hazarding a guess where you should go."

"We can help you get across the border," interrupted one of the smugglers. He twisted a finger through his beard, freeing a hail of crumbs that gathered on the toes of his shoes.

"Sure, no problem," said another. "Since you guys are friends of Sam, we'll take you both across for, let's say, 200 lira per man."

I didn't have the money, but even if I did, I would have had doubts about accepting their offer. Some of these guys would legitimately provide a service like this for cash, but very few would follow through if they knew they could get more for delivering a Westerner to the government or to a group of Islamists looking for a bartering chip to get their incarcerated buddies back. I didn't have anything against trusting locals when I had time to get to know them. But we'd just met these guys, and they were a little too eager to help out.

"You guys take Discover? How about traveler's checks? You're into bartering, right? How about you take us to Turkey in exchange for the right to name Kailas's firstborn daughter?"

"Page is twenty-three years old, Cogar," Kailas reminded.

"They didn't know that. Besides, Page is a sweet kid, and I'm sure she would agree to a name change if she knew it would get her dad and Uncle Cogar out of a pinch."

"So you have no money?" a smuggler asked. He didn't appear amused.

"I have some," Kailas said, fishing out his wallet. "I don't have any lira, but if you take dollars—"

I snatched his wallet and pretended to search its contents. "Not enough, I'm afraid. So onward we go, on foot. Thanks for lunch, guys. Keep up the good fight."

Kailas wrestled his wallet out of my hands and glowered, though he was smart enough to avoid arguing about it in their presence. Maybe he was beginning to learn that I didn't do this sort of thing flippantly; if my behavior seemed uncharacteristically odd, there was usually a reason for it.

Sam walked us to the door.

"You might want to lie low until it gets dark out," he warned. "I don't want to find your possessions on one of Assad's pigs."

I slipped off my boot, withdrew a crumpled 50 Turkish lira note—the last I had—and handed it to our guide, shaking his hand. "Hey, thanks for the meal. And, you know, for not killing us."

Smirking as he slid a rust-speckled Czech CZ-82 pistol from his belt, the sniper shoved it against my chest and said, "For the love of god, Mr. Cogar, take a gun with you."

"Yeah, okay," I said, accepting the handgun and holding it by my side, not wanting to argue with him or insult his generosity.

After saying our goodbyes and wishing them all the best, Kailas and I set out on our own again.

As we stepped into a narrow alleyway outside, blinking away the light from the smoke-veiled sun after spending hours in the dark of the mosque basement, Kailas said, "I noticed that you introduced yourself as a journalist, Cogar. Even when he asked if you were an aid worker, you said you worked for the *Herald*."

"Old habit."

"You sure that's it?"

"Of course I'm sure. It wouldn't matter what I said, anyway. We just needed for them not to kill us. Mission accomplished. Now let's go."

"You sure are a petulant fucker," Kailas grumbled, working a fingernail between his teeth to free the trapped lasagna.

I smirked, withdrew the pistol from my belt, dropped the magazine, cleared the chamber, and tossed it into the deep ashes inside a smoldering 50-gallon burn barrel. Melted plastic from wire sheathing bubbled on the rim. The copper wire would be dug out of the ashes later and sold in Turkey.

Kailas glanced inside the barrel. "You sure it's such a good idea to lose the gun?"

"Journalists don't carry guns," I said.

"But you're not a journalist, remember?"

"Old habit."

We continued our trek, navigating over the rubble and slipping into a nearby apartment complex with thin carpet in the hallways and the same moldy, airless musk of the inside of a hockey player's gear bag. But, like a centuries-old house built in the middle of Tornado Alley, this building was one of those statistical anomalies that hadn't acquired so much as a scratch during the war, even as the buildings around it fell.

"Let's rest until nightfall. We should be able to get around more safely in the dark," I said, gently knocking on the first door on the second floor. Swinging it open, I said, "C'est la honeymoon suite."

We entered and I took a quick look around to ensure we were alone. I always dreaded the thought of boldly kicking my way into some poor family's last refuge, causing them further distress because I'd been too dense to realize the place wasn't uninhabited.

Satisfied that we were free of company, I scooted a tattered recliner—the threadbare velvet fabric covering the arms pocked by cigarette burns—toward the window and gazed outside. A vulture lazily circled the adjoining courtyard.

"Fucking birds," I said.

Kailas peeked into the apartment's empty bedroom. "What do you have against birds? I would think you'd be happy to see any wildlife in a place as desolate as this."

"It's just that they're always watching," I said, sitting down, pushing up the chair's footrest, and unfolding the copy of the *Herald* that Sam had given me. "Just patiently observing, waiting to see what kind of meal they can get out of the day's fighting. You'll get no hand-wringing out of them, just cold apathy and greedy expectation. And I can't go a day without seeing them. You shuffle off to take a shit, there's one perched on a power pole, watching you drop trou. You slip your clothes off to wash up, the one from before brought a friend to watch. Voyeuristic little fuckers. And did you know vultures don't even have birdy vocal cords?" I lifted my chin and tapped my Adam's apple. "So they don't sing. They just hiss and grunt like some mute, flatulent taxi driver."

Kailas began rummaging through the kitchen cabinets in hopes of finding something to eat or drink. Judging by the layer of dust covering every horizontal surface in the room, the original inhabitants had left months before.

I sighed and unfolded my paper. "Letters to the editor. That should be entertaining."

My smile faded as I began reading, and Kailas asked, "What? That doesn't look entertaining to me."

"It's not." I scanned the short letter, reread it, and slammed the footrest home as I stood up. "This…reader, if you can call her that, called my last article 'poorly researched and an affront to honest journalism.' She actually had the gall to ask if I'd even been to Egypt. How could you let this run?"

Kailas nodded knowingly, recalling the content of the letter. "Like you said, it's entertaining. Readers eat this shit up."

"All right, you want entertaining? I'm going to write a rebuttal, and you're going to print it. Right? I at least deserve a chance to defend myself. Probably one of the assholes from the *Tribune* writing in under a pseudonym, anyway." I tore the article from the paper and let the rest fall to the floor.

"Am I going to have to redact this letter of yours to make it suitable for print?" Kailas asked, flipping the lever on the kitchen sink. Dry.

"You tell me. Am I allowed to call her a vacuous sack of afterbirth and the macabre result of a reckless and morally reprehensible exchange of reproductive fluids? No curse words, so it's fair game, right?"

Kailas leaned against the kitchen counter. "What happened to you, Cogar?" His tone had changed. He actually sounded concerned.

"What do you mean?"

"When I first got here, I could tell you were in a bad mood, a little shaken up, maybe, but I wasn't really worried about you. You were the same old bulletproof Cogar. Laugh off a near miss, chug a beer, chase some tail, and you're good. But these clumsy, rambling insults...that's not you. Where's the pointed, biting wit? For a man who finds sarcasm as much a compulsion as a defense mechanism, even thrives on it, that tells me something else is going on upstairs. Are you okay?"

I paused, retracing our conversations in search of examples. I had no idea what he was talking about. I was as sharp as I'd ever been. Wasn't I?

"I'm fine. Are you going to print this or not?" I asked, ignoring his attempt at counseling.

Kailas shook his head and sighed. He knew he wasn't going to get anywhere by pressing the point. "You know I'm not going to print this. Even if it was the most elegantly written collection of insults ever conceived, I'm not going to diminish the legitimacy of my newspaper or your career by indulging your sudden obsession with retaliating against one bored reader. It's an op-ed column, Cogar. It's not as though there haven't been others like this."

"There have? Just how many?" I shouted. This was news to me. I always assumed everyone loved me. Well, at least my readers. Okay, *most* of my readers.

"Do you even read our newspaper?" Kailas asked, staring at his palms as he realized the counter he'd been leaning against was covered in something sticky.

"The *Herald?* Of course not. With the exception of my stuff—of which I'm intimately familiar—there's nothing worth reading in there."

Looking for something to wipe his hands on, Kailas said, "You keep talking like that and you'll become intimately familiar with the classifieds section."

The sound of men yelling from the courtyard below interrupted our bickering. I looked out the window to find a family surrounded by enormous, steroid-inflated, black-clad men armed with machetes.

"Kailas, you ever just have one of those days...." I said nervously, pocketing the offending newspaper article and shuffling out of the soldiers' line of sight, peeking out the window from cover.

"What do you mean? Who are those guys?" he asked.

"It's the Shabiha."

"What's that?" Kailas whispered, moving beside me and looking down into the courtyard. I grabbed his shirt collar and pulled him away from the window.

"Assad's Ghosts. The president's mercenary death squad."

10
Shabiha

One of the behemothic, bearded men swung the handle of his machete into a dark-haired man's temple. Another grabbed at a teenage girl, wrapping his meaty arm—covered in large tattoos of President Assad's likeness—around her waist as he dragged her to a wall, pinned her in place, and began pawing at her clothes. Kailas pulled at his hair.

"We've got to do something, Cogar." He wiped at tears as he pleaded. I'd never seen him so upset. Furious? Plenty of times. Tearful? Never.

But I knew that seeing such viciousness leveled at a young woman was hitting him hard; his youngest daughter, Julie, had just turned eighteen.

"Like what?" I whispered. "We haven't got a gun. Unless you want us to die, too—"

"We had a gun, dammit. You threw it away," he said, grabbing a handful of my shirt and shaking me.

I slapped his hand away. "One rusty Eastern Bloc pistol against a patrol of Assad's most bloodthirsty men would be about as good as throwing down against a biker gang while armed with a Red Rider and a riding crop. Kailas, there's nothing we can do for them. I'm sorry. I wish it was different, but getting yourself killed isn't going to save those people, it'll just leave your kids without a father."

"We have to do something!" Kailas shouted.

The sound carried through the open window and down to the courtyard, the mercenaries looking up in unison.

"Oh, you dense fucker," I growled as I eyed their reaction, punching my mentor's chest.

The men yelled to one another in Arabic, all but one charging for us through the open doorway below.

"Kailas, hide."

Without looking at my mentor, I sprinted out of the room, down the hallway with the thin carpet, until I reached the building's end and squeezed through an open window.

"I know you were doing all right before, Cogar, but I thought I'd just show up in the middle of a war, clueless, and force you into a fight with a gang of brobdingnagian, juiced-up sociopaths. Hope you're cool with that," I said mockingly to myself as I planted my boots on a narrow ledge outside the window.

Taking a shallow breath, I looked down to the cracked pavement several stories below, and then to a fire escape dangling from the adjacent building. I leapt into the air, my fingers wrapping around the bottommost steel rung. For a second, I thought I'd made it. The loud snap of the fragile weld holding the bar in place stunned me almost as much as the twenty-foot fall onto the roof of the mercenaries' minibus parked below.

Groaning and stretching my back, I looked over just in time to see the mercenary tasked with guarding the civilians leap from the ground toward me, his machete cocked back, ready to bury it in my neck. I rolled away. His blade plunged through the vehicle's thin aluminum skin inches from my skull. In return for the man's unwarranted aggression, I whipped the ladder rung still in my grip against his wrist. Crying out in pain as he released his blade, the thug jumped back from the van and began calling out for his companions as their captives beat an urgent escape.

Sliding off the vehicle, I began walking toward the mercenary slowly, letting the pipe hang at my side.

"I've never understood that," I said, my eyes narrow and my head down. "Your type gets their jollies from hurting other people—make your living by inflicting pain—but when the tables are turned, you turn into gutless cowards. You'd think a guy who lives by the sword wouldn't be so quick to cower when the blade gets turned on him."

After looking once more toward the building where his friends had entered, the Ghost seemed to realize he was on his own. The big man growled and rushed me, his colossal frame bent forward at the waist.

I stood my ground. This, I thought, must be how a big game hunter feels staring down a charging bull elephant. Inside me raged a battle, my every instinct demanding that I flee while my mind insisted that if I tried, he'd trample me. I swallowed hard, gripped the steel bar in my hand a little harder, and forced myself to stay put.

When he'd closed to within a few feet, I swung the ladder rung like a club, twisting at the torso and moving the energy from my hips through my arms to my wrists. The pipe collided with my assailant's chin. His eyes rolled back in his head, arms dropping limply to his sides, knees striking the dirt, and he collapsed at my feet.

"Line drive, shallow centerfield, and the folks in the crowd are just losing their minds out here," I announced in my best broadcaster's voice, dropping my impromptu weapon on the unconscious brute's barrel chest and taking a jog around imaginary bases surrounding my fallen foe.

Turning to look at the building, wondering how I was going to retrieve Kailas without the mercenaries seeing me, my heart sank. They'd heard the commotion and had begun emerging from the doorway, each man larger and more intimidating than the last. Looking from me to their fallen comrade, they didn't even bother to draw their sidearms.

They were going to make me suffer.

"Now, you guys look like you all weightlift quite a bit," I said, holding my hands up passively. "But how's your cardio?"

Turning on a heel, I sprinted into a narrow alleyway adjacent to the courtyard. I'd just have to come back for Kailas after I'd lost these guys.

Daring a glance over my shoulder, my heart rate tripled as I spotted one of the men moving his 250-pound frame fast enough to gain on me, his heavy footfalls thundering against the pavement as he kicked through the twisted bits of tin and garbage scattered throughout the alley.

"Really wish I'd eaten my Wheaties this morning," I puffed, turning a sharp corner. A blur swung toward my head, and I narrowly managed to dodge its impact. I looked back to see Kailas, a length of steel guide rail in his hands, bury the pipe against my follower's sternum. Stumbling and gasping for air, the bearded mercenary fumbled for a Glock pistol stuffed in his belt. Before he could level the weapon at either of us, I grabbed the Ghost's wrist with my left hand, the pistol's slide with my right, and twisted the gun to face his forearm. No amount of steroid-bolstered muscle could overcome the anatomical impossibility of holding on to an object with one's wrist bent 180 degrees backward.

Relieving the mercenary of his weapon, I fired a quick round at his knee in the hopes of incapacitating him. I missed by no small margin and hit him squarely in the groin.

I winced as he screamed, clutching wildly at his manhood. I grabbed Kailas by the shirt collar and shoved him down the alley.

"Feel like going for a run?"

"Not especially," he said. Realizing he was still holding the guide rail, Kailas let it drop to the pavement.

"Well you're about to set a new personal best on the quarter mile, old pal." I urged him forward, pistol trained on the corner where the others would soon emerge.

"You're keeping the gun this time, right?" Kailas asked.

"Yes. This time I'm keeping the fucking gun."

11
Make-Believe Messiah

"What you did back there was pretty impressive," Kailas said as we resumed our trek, now several blocks off course and thoroughly disoriented following our hasty escape from the Ghosts. "You must have balls of steel to face down one of those bruisers with only a metal pipe for a weapon. I would have run."

"You saw that, huh?" I laughed. "Truth is, I'm a coward. But as a coward, I'm also afraid to die, so sometimes I do things that could be misconstrued as bravery while trying to save my own skin."

We entered what appeared to have once been a railway yard. Stepping between ties and broken tracks, we skirted the station complex along its arcade. A few of the arched windows, like those of a gothic cathedral, retained their original stained glass, but none were without bullet holes or missing panes. The entire scene possessed a gloomy malaise that seemed better suited to a Neo-classical oil painting than to reality.

Kailas glanced at me and cleared his throat. "I'm sorry I forced you into that situation back there, but we couldn't just let those people be killed. I'm surprised at you, frankly. Here you're going on and on about your "duty" and "making a difference here." But you were really prepared to let those people die, weren't you?"

My vision narrowed, and I felt an irrepressible rage building. Grabbing my mentor by his shirtfront, I slammed him against the building's limestone wall.

"Kailas, you're an anemic, toothless gift horse dropped into my lap like a crying child with a full diaper. If it'd just been me, I would have gladly thrown my life away trying to save them," I growled. "But I owe it to your wife and kids to see that you get back to Chicago in one piece. Getting myself killed is one thing, but come Hell or high water, I'm getting you out of here alive. Understand?"

I gave him a final shake and continued walking, stepping into the shadows of a barrel vault that cut between two of the station's buildings. I slipped on an empty glass Coke bottle, caught myself, turned, and punted it into the wall.

Watching the bottle as it skidded along the brick, Kailas cleared his throat, re-tucked his shirt, and rolled his shoulder. "Look, I'm sorry Cogar. This is all new to me. I don't make life-or-death decisions. Ever."

I stopped, standing beneath one of the tunnel's skylights and looked up, resting my hands on the back of my head. The sun obstinately hung behind clouds and smoke.

"They don't get easier," I said, my voice echoing in the narrow tunnel. I could tell I'd hurt his feelings; as gruff as he was, I'd known Kailas long enough to be able to tell when something was troubling him. "Hey, you did good back there, too," I forced myself to sound encouraging. "That was handy work with that steel pipe. Couldn't have timed it better."

Kailas shuffled. "Actually, I was aiming for you and just happened to hit the right guy."

I frowned.

"What? How was I supposed to know it was you?" he asked, raising his arms.

"I was the smaller guy that looked like an American."

"You look like a hoodlum."

"What a grumpy, old man thing to say."

"Well, I've got plenty to be grumpy about lately." Kailas reached a hand over his shoulder, blindly feeling for his flipped shirt collar. "Everything here is so twisted, so brutal. Makes a guy surly."

"I've actually thought of a way to fix that," I said, gesturing for him to follow as I continued through the tunnel. The trash left on the uneven brick floor and the astringent stink of urine emanating from the drains underfoot gave the impression that someone had been living here, likely hiding out beneath the century-old stone in hopes of surviving Assad's artillery. I wondered what, or who, had driven them out.

"Oh yeah?" Kailas played along. "Do share."

"Well, it won't fix those meatheads from the Shabiha—they've probably got balls the size of raisins after all the gym candy they've shot up, and obviously get their jollies staring at photos of Assad—but I figure it would subdue those jihadist-types that had a gun to your head when you first got here. What we really need is a boatload of skin mags. Musty garage-sale classics should work just fine. Actually, we should be air-dropping in entire printing presses so we can better generate the volume necessary to calm those guys down."

"They do not need pornography," Kailas scolded.

"No really, they do. They can't be trusted with women or goats, so paper will have to do. They have all this pent-up, repressed sexual energy coming out sideways. Too bad Allah didn't think of that when he was slapping together the rulebook."

"Religion is the only thing that keeps places like this together, Cogar. Imagine a world without laws, if everyone did like you say and gave in to their natural urges."

"Come on, you know as well as I do that religion can be twisted to accommodate any nefarious thing people put their minds to," I said. "Look around; how many women and children have been killed in the name of

Allah? How many soldiers have surrendered to a religious man, only to have their head cut off with a blunt knife?"

"That's a bastardization of religion, Cogar. Not a good example."

"Oh come on, why are you defending this? I know you don't believe in any of that man-in-the-sky bullshit."

"I go to church every Sunday."

I turned, drew an imaginary sword from my hip, and with an exaggerated flourish, swung it toward him, shouting, "Genuflect, heathen!" He recoiled. I laughed. "You only go because Dannielle makes you."

"And because I believe in something greater than myself," he insisted.

"Kailas, do you have any idea how many men I've seen die clutching crosses, or mumbling the Shahada as they bled out? Do you know how many of those prayers helped? Not one. Because there's no one listening. There's you, and me, and the sky above, and the dirt below. When we die, the lights go out, and that's all she wrote. Besides, no god but a twisted, perverted one would allow the world to look like this. It's easy for religious types who go to church on Sunday and return to mow their lawn in their suburban neighborhood to declare there's a greater purpose or some such platitudinous nonsense, but the fact remains that your God apparently only looks after lottery winners and athletes. If these religious mental asylum escapees realized that this life was all they got, they'd be a whole lot less eager to blow themselves up in the name of Allah."

That got Kailas fired up. He began tugging his sleeves up to his elbows, but got stuck trying to undo the buttons on his wrists. "You're full of bluster and bravado, Cogar, but admit it, even you have begged for salvation out there. Like they say, there are no atheists in foxholes."

"Kailas, I have prayed for only two things in my entire life: for Julie Clark in the eleventh grade to wear a miniskirt while taking the stairs a few steps ahead of me, and for me not to die ingloriously on the toilet. So far, if there is a god, he's delivered only one of those two, and there's still time for him to go back on that."

I knelt to lace up my boot as Kailas continued walking, shouting at me over his shoulder as he went.

"Yeah? Well explain how you just happened to be passing by at the exact moment that I was about to be shot. Those are impossible odds. Five minutes earlier or later, and you never would have even known I'd been here. If that's not a sign that God's looking out for the both of us...."

He exited the tunnel and strolled out into the adjoining street with the same negligent abandon as a sparrow plunging like a Stuka dive bomber toward a large plate glass window. If such a bird could have a human expression as it fitfully spasmed on the lawn, waiting for the homeowner to retrieve a shovel from the garden shed, it would have mirrored the one Kailas wore at that moment.

There were shouts. Kailas turned to look at me as he placed his hands atop his head.

No. Don't stop there. Run, dammit.

He'd walked directly into a government mobile checkpoint. That was why the refugees who had been staying here were gone. They'd caught wind of the approaching soldiers or had been driven off by them.

"It's okay, I'm a journalist," I heard him shout as the guards approached, the muzzles of their rifles rising level with his chest.

No one here cared that he was a journalist. You didn't get a free pass from Assad just because you weren't an active participant in the war efforts, and there were thousands of dead NGO workers, medical personnel, and reporters to prove it. The president had a pretty good idea about containment and keeping a political advantage, and it began and ended with killing anyone who might get a compassionate or humiliating story out of the country.

Kailas's knees were kicked out from behind him, his arms wrestled behind his back and a plastic zip tie tightened around his wrists. Suddenly realizing that his entreaties were falling on deaf ears, he began cursing at his captors with the kind of stunning creativity I'd always admired him for.

"What, you get tired of playing with each others' conspicuously shrimp-sized dicks, you inbred, sex-shop-changing-room-seat-sniffing bastards? You feeling threatened by a lowly American journalist, you post-coital circumcisions? What a bunch of chicken-shit, wide-stance urinal users. I'm not afraid of you. Fuck you. And you, fuck him. And you, watch and take notes. Cocksuckers."

They dragged him away, the slacks he'd worked so hard to keep clean tearing at the knees as they passed over sharp rocks and shattered asphalt. Before he passed out of sight, he turned his head and looked at me. Though defiant, there was a shade of apology in his eyes, and a subtle pleading.

Cogar, get me out of here.

Panic anchored me in place. After all I'd promised Kailas, I'd just let him walk out into the middle of the street and get captured. I felt like a parent who had just let their clumsy, guileless child take a tumble down a staircase. I should have kept a better eye on him. I knew better.

"Come on, Cogar. You sit still now, and you'll never see Kailas again. You promised you'd get him home," I said to myself as I tried to conjure a plan.

I snuck into the street, looking for a better vantage point. Ascending the crumbling stone façade of a nearby building, I watched as Kailas was forced into the bed of a waiting armored personnel carrier and driven away. To where, I had no idea. And that terrified me.

But what really made my blood turn cold was the regime soldier pointing a finger at me, a rocket-propelled grenade launcher resting on his other shoulder.

"*Ashouf kaman!*" he yelled to his comrades as he sighted down the length of the launcher's tube.

I hurled myself off the precipice, landing on the building's earthen floor a story below just as the anti-tank grenade struck the concrete above me. Stone and rubble rained down. Darkness followed.

****

Port-au-Prince, Haiti
January 2010

Haiti was paradise made hellish, a contemporary Pompeii. Weeks after the massive earthquake shattered the country, survivors, hundreds of thousands of them, squirmed in ant-like colonies beneath wind-ragged tarpaulins, sun-bleached floral bed sheets, and clumsily nailed-together tin. Some NGO group had gotten the brilliant idea to ship in hundreds of Conex containers for use as shelters, but they sat empty; the Caribbean sun superheated the steel boxes until no one could stand to be inside them. There were plenty of Americans and Europeans about, helping with clean-up and administering basic medical care, but the latrines were still being dug too close to the refugee camps, the dead still being piled in the streets, and the undertakers still only covering their mouth and nose with their tee shirts when carrying out decaying bodies.

That wasn't why I was there. Stories about the quake and its impact on the already poor inhabitants had been written. Charities had been founded. Celebrities had selected this particular disaster as one for which they'd make their annual appeal to the American middle class for support. Televised fundraising concerts were scheduled. Relief workers and journalists flooded into the small country. But I had found a story that the outside world hadn't been exposed to yet.

Haiti was, even before the earthquake, a fragile, corrupt state, run less by politicians than by gangs. These gangs were so powerful, they were viewed by the locals as communities or political organizations rather than bands of roving thugs. But between the hysteria brought on by the disaster, the influx of wealthy, well-meaning-but-clueless Westerners ripe for kidnapping, and the collapse of the prisons and subsequent escape of thousands of inmates, the gangs had swelled to their most powerful, and their most active.

A week before, I had written a letter to Joseph Appolon, leader of the ex-FADH—a gang made up of disbanded Haitian Army soldiers—asking for a meeting and interview. To my surprise, he sent me a prompt reply. It was written on a sun-yellowed sheet of paper bearing his 'official' title and the ex-FADH's seal. I had this guy pegged. His eager response, his pretentious letterhead, Appolon was no different than the hundreds of other rebel-faction and gang leaders I'd interviewed over the years. He was trying to project power and gain legitimacy by having his words and likeness showcased in a Western publication. That worked for me; those kinds of men embrace journalists and will usually go well out of their way to give them access to an interview.

From my research, I'd learned that Appolon was all about promoting the return of the Duvalierist military, hoping Haiti's next government would reinstitute the armed forces to which he once belonged. With so many reporters in the country, he'd seen an opportunity. I just happened to be the first to reach out to him. I flew out the next day.

His man was supposed to meet me at the Azitlan Bar at noon. It was a dumpy little place, just one small room, airless and humid. The old American beer posters on the walls had turned yellow and curled at the corners. The tables and chairs were sticky and rocked on an uneven floor, but I suspected it had been that way long before the earthquake. An hour passed. I stacked half a dozen empty glasses on the table in front of me, the locally distilled sugarcane rum blurring my sight. I was sweaty, bored, drunk, and had to pee. And still, no sign of my contact. Some men fear being stood up by blind dates. I feared being stood up by nervous sources I'd flown 1,800 miles to meet.

"Excuse me," I waved at the bartender. He took my gesture to mean I wanted another drink and began dumping more of the amber liquid into a fresh glass. "No, no, that's...fine." I stood and approached the bar, slamming the fresh drink and covering the glass with my palm to keep him from filling it again. "Where's the bathroom? Um, la toilette?"

The bartender pointed outside. "Il est à l'extérieur."

"It's out there?"

The man stepped out from behind the bar, made a gesture like withdrawing his member from his pants and urinating on a wall, and then pointed at the back of the building.

Plumbing. Who needs it?

I flipped a twenty onto the bar and stepped outside. Garbage and merchants lined the streets. The air smelled of feces and diesel smoke. A light-duty pickup truck, bed packed with a dozen people and their belongings, motored by. I unzipped my pants. A man sitting on the sidewalk a block away, hands sweeping pebbles back and forth between his legs, caught my eye, nodded, and gestured for me to follow him. Either he had seen me unzip my fly and had gotten the wrong impression about what kind of guy I was, or my point of contact had misunderstood my very explicit directions to meet me inside the bar.

He didn't give his name. He didn't say anything at all. The man just led on, through back alleys, dry creek beds lined with broken glass and loose trash, and a small encampment where the women hung laundry to dry and the men lounged in the shade, gathered around an antique television resting on a milk crate. My guide walked as though he wore shoes a size too small—his strides short and urgent.

"We're going to see Joseph Appolon, right?" I asked.

"Appolon. Oui. Appolon." He rolled back a piece of chain-link fence and urged me ahead, then passed me as we began marching up the pie-crust terrain leading to another small settlement on a hill—this one slightly more developed than the refugee camps swirling into the valleys below. We approached a concrete shell of a building—no windows—and entered. I followed my guide up a flight of stairs and suddenly found myself in the company of a group of very hard-looking, impassive men. At their center, a potbellied man in a U.S. Navy t-shirt anxiously massaged his thin moustache.

"Monsieur Appolon?" I asked, offering my hand.

He stared at me doubtfully for a moment. An oscillating fan teased the edges of a stack of blank papers on the man's desk. I was suddenly very cognizant of the heat.

"Your zipper is undone, Monsieur Cogar." The room erupted in laughter.

Relieved, I fixed my fly and shook his hand. Sweaty, his sausage-like fingers wrapped too low on my fingers during the gesture, pinching them together and making it impossible for me to give anything but a feeble shake in return. Joseph grinned and offered me a seat.

"I appreciate your willingness to meet with me on such short notice," I said as I reached into my leather duffel bag. "I brought you a gift." I withdrew an unopened bottle of duty-free bourbon and a handful of tactical self-defense pens—the kind meant to be used as a Kubotan or striking tool while still passing for a writing apparatus. Weapons, regardless of how gimmicky or effectively useless they might be, held a universal appeal to men the world over. And whether dealing with a white-collar Westerner or a tribesman wearing a loincloth, gifts surpass language and culture. Thoughtfulness, even in the form of some cheap crap that most people would discard in the States, went miles in gaining a host's trust and ingratiating oneself.

The men in the room beamed as they passed around the pens, making stabbing motions at one another, and Appolon wasted no time in opening the bottle of whiskey.

"You mind if I shoot a couple of photos?" I asked.

"Not at all," Joseph said, sliding open his desk drawer. Withdrawing a MAC-10 machine pistol, Joseph leaned back in his chair, held the gun in the air, and donned a wolfish expression. Every third-world tough knew to keep photo props on hand.

After a few dozen photos, I tossed my camera back inside my bag before anyone got the idea to take it from me. Photo shoot over,

Joseph carelessly dropped the MAC-10 on his desktop, and I took a sharp breath as it clattered to the wood, stubby barrel pointed at my chest. I'd seen plenty of third-world weapons with worn-out sears go off when dropped, and Joseph didn't strike me as someone who had ever bothered to maintain his gun or have it looked at by a gunsmith.

"So, as we spoke about, can I ask you a few questions?" I asked, placing my voice recorder on Joseph's desk and withdrawing my notepad.

"Oui, uh, yes. Yes, ask anything."

"Let's start with the local police. What's your relationship with them? It looks to me as though they let your men do as they please."

Joseph took a deep swig of the bourbon before answering. "The police won't come to this area. They fear us, as well they should. This is our country. We know what's best for our people."

"It's widely known that your organization, and others like it here, funds its operations with money gained from prostitution and human trafficking. Yet you argue you're helping your countrymen. Do they share your outlook? Or are people resentful?"

Joseph glanced at his men, squirmed in his seat, and said, "Monsieur Cogar, if the earthquake had swallowed up only the gangs, there would still be crime. We've simply become the face of it. We are the only ones keeping order here. Did you see any policemen outside today?"

"Not many," I admitted.

"Yes, most have run home to their families. Which is just as well, since they do little even when they are working. The streets, with or without them, would be chaos if not for us. The police are poodles barking from behind their master's leg. The masters, the

politicians, turn to us to keep the wolves from coming inside. This is our country." He emphasized those final words by poking the desktop with his pointer finger. His men nodded like dashboard bobbleheads.

"This control you have over the country's politicians—is that the reason you feel you own the country? It's no secret that Haitian politicians rely on groups like yours for protection, for blackmail, for exerting influence, and in some cases, just getting elected."

Joseph returned to the bottle, the booze slipping from the corners of his mouth and dribbling down his chin as his motor skills dulled. He wiped his chin and smiled. "The politicians know who really run this country. If they want something, they know who to ask. They pay us for their privilege."

"When I spoke to the communications director at the U.N. mission's intelligence center, he said—" I flipped to another page of my notebook. "'As long as crime remains as pervasive as it is in Haiti, and as long as gangs are able to act with complete impunity, rebuilding the country's infrastructure is a fool's errand.'"

"Fool's errand? Je ne comprends pas. I, uh, don't understand that expression," Joseph said, scooting his chair closer to his desk.

"Something pointless. Ineffective."

"Well I would say the U.N. is pointless and ineffective."

Of course he would say that. But we both knew that the only thing preventing Haiti from sliding into a full-on Mad-Max-style free-for-all was the U.N. They were the thin, languid muscle that held the shattered skeleton of the country together, however clumsily they might have done it.

Someone coughed from the hallway behind me. I turned to see an old man, gray haired and with a dark splotch of scar tissue, like a *puddle of oil on asphalt, covering his neck. He gesticulated angrily at Joseph, beckoning him to the hallway.*

The commander excused himself and withdrew from the room, stumbling over a chair leg, and then his own legs. Judging by the reverence paid to the old man by the armed guards nearby, and given Joseph's sudden cowed demeanor, I figured he was an authority within the gang's hierarchy. The old guy looked pissed, gesturing wildly toward where I sat, speaking in rapid-fire French. Despite the room's fans, the afternoon heat plastered my shirt to my back. The bottle of bourbon had been drained. No one spoke, but I was glared at whenever I stood to leave. I'd gotten my story, my quotations, a few photos. Get me on a plane, get me back to the States.

I didn't like that Joseph had known I was coming to see him for days. He'd had time to think about what to do with me. My apprehension had initially been put to rest when he'd agreed to an interview; I figured he was getting what he wanted—publicity— and I was getting what I wanted—my story. Everyone wins. But their refusal to let me leave, and the tension that seemed to be increasing with each silent moment, had me fearing the worst.

Finally, Joseph returned, slumping into his seat. I wasted no time.

"I've got to be getting back to my hotel. My flight leaves soon. I appreciate your time, Joseph."

"Je suis désolé, Monsieur Cogar. I can't let you leave," he said, face covered in beads of sweat he refused to wipe away. "I've been told you intend to write, eh, négatif things about me and my men."

He was testing me. I kept calm and answered, "I haven't even put pen to paper yet. I'm only researching. You've got nothing to hide, anyway, right?" Put the ball back in his court.

"I have nothing to hide," he agreed.

"See? Look, I'll send you a draft of what I've written before it goes to print, okay? That way you can decide if it's accurate," I lied.

"I don't think you'll have the means to do that," he said sadly. Two guards approached, one drawing a rusty machete from a sheath at his belt, the other lunging and wrapping his forearm around my neck, pinning me against the backrest of my chair.

I struggled to free myself as the machete-wielding gangster raised his weapon.

"No, Joseph, please. This isn't how you want to make the news. It's not worth it," I said, jamming my foot against the desk in an attempt to flip my chair.

A shiver ran through my seat. A rolling stampede of car alarms cried in the distance. Moving closer. Becoming louder. The walls of the building vibrated. The ceiling coughed dust. Everyone in the room froze, staring at one another with wild-eyed surprise as they reached for anything solid to hold onto, the tremors from the aftershock becoming more violent. The floor gave way beneath me, the ceiling following me down.

Above the chalky crumble of dislocated masonry, I heard a whisper.

They range the field and they rove the flood,
And they climb the mountain's crest;
Theirs is the curse of the gypsy blood,
And they don't know how to rest.

12
In the Hot Seat
Aleppo, Syria
June 2013

The haze cleared. Shoving bits of brick and dusty stone away from my face, I crawled out of the rubble. My shirt was torn from my shoulder to my hip, my forearms and face covered in a patchwork of lacerations. A sizeable bruise began to form on my abdomen, and my ears rang with the sound of a thousand pissed-off mosquitoes. But I was alive. Still, I had no time to nurse my wounds or recover. I needed to get Kailas back before he got thrown into one of the regime prisons or ended up 'disappeared' in an even more permanent fashion.

The rumble of a car grabbed my attention. I shook off the dizziness and achingly moved until I could see into the street. After a few seconds, a vehicle—more motorcycle than automobile—rolled into view. One of Assad's soldiers approached, his rifle slung across the handlebars. Turning into the alley separating the building I was in from the next, he stopped, parked the bike, and walked into a nearby alcove—unzipping his pants and shuffling them to his thighs. I followed, waiting until he'd laid his rifle on the ground and sat down to shit before I made my move. I scooped up his gun. Checked the action. He scrambled to pull up his pants.

"English?" I asked. My head was throbbing.

He fastened his belt and puffed his chest, eying the rifle. "Fuck you."

"I'll take that as a resounding yes. Here's the deal, I need to know where your buddies are taking my friend." I let the muzzle drift toward the man's torso.

"As I said, fuck you."

"That's not very polite." I took a deep breath, careful to keep my tone calm and dispassionate. "Look, I'm not typically a violent man. In fact, I've gone well out of my way to be a neutral observer in this fucked-up little war you and your buddies started. That said, you just kidnapped a very dear friend of mine. The closest friend I have in this world. And believe me when I tell you that I would go to any lengths to save him. If you don't tell me where, exactly, they are taking him, I will empty this rifle's magazine into your face. I will aerate your skull until I'm able to piss on your corpse and water the grass."

The man only laughed defiantly.

So I nodded and chuckled with him before I butt-stroked him in the jaw with his own gun.

He groaned and spat blood and broken teeth. I dragged him by the hair through the doorway of a deserted restaurant. Propping him up on one of the plastic chairs in a corner, I pulled off his boots, tugged out the laces, and used them to lash his wrists to the chair's arms. Taking a step into the kitchen, I grabbed a pile of dirty washrags, a kerosene lantern, and a matchbook.

I knew what needed to be done if I wanted to get Kailas back. It was time to get ruthless. As a man who made his living communicating with words, I sometimes forgot that the levels of communication went far deeper than speech. The time for negotiation had passed. It was time to show this guy, in explicit detail, that I meant business. I cracked my knuckles.

"It's a bit chilly in here, don't you think?" I asked, tossing the rags on the floor beneath the soldier's chair. Methodically unscrewing the cap from the lamp's fuel reservoir, I splashed the kerosene over the rags. I lit a match and held it in front of the man's bloodied nose as he bobbed in and out of consciousness.

"Tell me where my friend is, and I'll blow this match out right now. I'll walk away and you'll never have to see my ugly face again."

Nothing.

The flame worked its way down the shaft of the matchstick, creeping toward my thumb and pointer finger on the opposite end.

"I don't want to drop this match, friend, but it's getting hot. Talk quickly, and you'll literally save your own ass."

The corners of his mouth pulled up into a weak grin. He spat, a mist of blood striking my face.

I waited until the heat stung my fingertips before I tossed the match into the pile of rags. A puff of flame enveloped him for only a second before the rags began burning more evenly, bright and hot, the flame licking the underside of his seat.

"That should warm you right up."

The man scooted around in panic, the fire nipping at his legs and melting through the chair's plastic seat. I planted a boot on the seat to keep him centered on the flame.

"Tell me where they're taking my friend, or you won't be able to shit without coating up with aloe vera." The smell of burning fabric and urine filled the small room.

"My men will tear out your insides," he groaned between clenched teeth.

Leaning back as casually as if I'd wandered off the street to listen to a live band, I said, "Don't worry, I can wait until you're ready to tell me."

His groans gave way to a pleading whine, his mouth open as if screaming. Drips of melted plastic hissed as they fell into the flame.

"You're running out of time to negotiate. This is only going to get more painful," I said, feeling my stomach heaving dangerously as the smell of seared flesh settled in my nose. I tried to maintain my impassive appearance, but I was ready to lose it. I'd been on the other side of torture, knew the terror and the agony more intimately than I would wish upon anyone. Never in my life could I have predicted that I'd be the one inflicting pain of this magnitude on another human being. It was repulsive, sickening. It would no doubt haunt my dreams as much as any other revolting scene from my past. Maybe a great deal more. But I had to get Kailas back, and I could think of no other way to do it. He'd braved Hell to come get me, and I would buy a beach house there if that's what it took to get him home.

After a few more seconds of fighting to keep his mouth shut, the soldier screamed, "The Sabbagh Estate security outpost! Al Assad Lake! Please!" He slammed his feet on the concrete floor, raising his pelvis in the air in an attempt to create distance between his seared ass and the heat.

I yanked his chair away from the flame, dumping him facedown on the floor. My mouth was salivating, my throat tightening, and my vision clouded by a fresh pool of tears. I swallowed hard and said, "I'm gonna borrow your bike. Good luck with the skin grafts."

Rushing outside, I took a desperate breath of fresh air. I wasn't proud of what I'd done, but I had an idea of where Kailas was, and that had made it worth it. At least for now.

As I approached the soldier's bike, I glanced up to the perch where I'd stood before the RPG had struck. An Egyptian vulture, a dirty-white crest of feathers fringing its mustard-yellow head, scooted along the windowsill, head hunched and wings tucked tight to its bulbous form.

"What are you looking at?" I shouted, picking up a stone and throwing it at the bird. The rock narrowly missed, but the creature didn't move. It only stared at me with an idle, indifferent look, dark eyes empty of emotion as it patiently waited for me to leave so it could investigate the smell of blistered flesh.

I felt the urge to kill it. To chase it down and wrap my hands around its miserable neck, to twist the squawking, flapping life from it. It had seen me drag the soldier inside, had heard the man's desperate, pleading cries. And as the evildoer emerged from within, this bird, in all its ostensible neutrality, only awaited its turn, fidgeting eagerly, doing little more than giving me a passing nod as I walked by. Sure, it was just a bird doing what it was programmed by nature to do. But there was already a glut of observers, crowds of hovering scavengers standing by in this war. It didn't need more.

Turning back to the motorcycle, I discovered that it wasn't a motorcycle at all, but rather a Nazi Kettenkrad halftrack—bullet-riddled and rusty, but still bearing the faint outline of a swastika on its fender. The aesthetic lovechild of a tank and a motorcycle, a Kettenkrad still seeing time on the battlefield would have made most military museum curators livid. Or sexually aroused.

Tossing my rifle into the halftrack's rear storage and searching its contents, I found a half-melted chocolate bar, a map, and a battery-powered radio. Thumbing over the map as I ripped open the chocolate, I pinpointed Al Assad Lake; following its shores, I found the penciled-in security outpost where they were holding Kailas. I was relieved my captive had spoken the truth; I didn't think I had it in me to go back inside that restaurant for another round of light the human candle.

Firing up the radio, I dialed in the FSA's pirate station. Creedence Clearwater Revival's "Fortunate Son" came on. I cranked the volume, started the vehicle up, and propped the radio between my knees. Candy bar hanging out of my mouth like a cigar, I aimed a middle finger at the still-watching vulture overhead and motored out of the alleyway.

13

Sameera

Al Assad Lake

Driving faster didn't mean I was any safer, but it made me feel a little better. I rumbled along the narrow streets, jostled as the Kettenkrad's front tire dipped into potholes and the dual tracks thrust me forward over stones and fallen concrete barriers. The buildings began to thin out, and I could finally see the security outpost in the distance, a speck on the shore of Al Assad Lake.

The encampment was fully equipped with an observation tower and machine gun nests, the shielded barrels of rolling anti-tank guns stuffed between gaps in the concrete blocks. Certain suicide if I were to approach on the halftrack. I pulled in the clutch and downshifted to neutral, letting the Kettenkrad coast down a small rise before abandoning it and approaching on foot. Crouched low behind a string of concrete road barriers, I contemplated how best to save Kailas. I drew the Glock from my belt, tugged back the slide until I spotted the glimmer of brass inside, and peeked over the top of the barrier.

I needed a uniform to covertly enter the area and, ideally, get close enough to rescue Kailas. The guards weren't going to give theirs up willingly. If I'd been back with my FSA contingent, I could have picked one out in my exact size from a pile they'd taken from regime soldiers over the years. But today I was on my own. Not that it would have mattered; it was a weak plan. It was one thing to pass for a rebel; after all, they didn't care if your story was bizarre—theirs probably was too. But Assad's regime was run like a legitimate army, and they weren't likely to fall for my playground-level antics.

Eyeing the razor-wire-ringed installation, I picked out the machine gun nests, looking for any area where they may have neglected to set up overlapping fields of fire. It was ironclad. No doubt the entire area had been sown with landmines, too.

Cursing, I returned to the Kettenkrad and began digging through the storage compartments looking for something that would jar a brilliant thought or strategy. I was rewarded with only a few nude pictures of an overweight, hirsute Syrian woman stuffed inside an ammo can alongside a few extra magazines for the rifle I'd taken from the bike's original rider.

That was the ticket.

Jamming the loaded magazines between the Kettenkrad's exhaust manifold and engine block, I started the engine and smashed the vehicle's Bakelite throttle housing. Pulling the loose throttle cable until the motor was revving loudly, I tied the cable around the handlebars, and standing to the bike's side, let go of the clutch. The Kettenkrad lurched forward, bearing straight down the road leading to the regime outpost. I didn't waste time watching it approach.

Racing perpendicular to the vehicle's path, I skirted around the outpost. As long as the machine gun nest covering my approach turned to fire on the Kettenkrad, I'd be free to close the distance, and ideally, rescue Kailas. If they didn't take the bait, I was pretty sure I'd know about it straightaway. There was just something about being shot at with a machine gun that made you instantly rethink your life choices.

The Kettenkrads' four-cylinder inline engine roared distantly. What followed was an erratic popping of gunshots—the rifle rounds I'd fastened to the halftrack igniting from the heat generated by the vehicle's exhaust.

Seconds later, apocalypse. World War III broke out as every submachine gun, rocket-propelled grenade launcher, recoilless rifle, and crew-served mounted

machine gun opened up on that poor antique vehicle—
the outpost thinking they were under assault.

Scrambling over a barricade, I sprinted toward the tall
concrete walls surrounding the outpost's central
building. Eyes fastened on the tower overlooking my
approach, I realized I'd underestimated the distance I
would need to cross. My legs burned, my chest heaving
as I kept pushing at a full sprint. The second the barrel
of that machine gun turned my way, it was game over. I
dropped my rifle to quicken my pace. If it came down to
a shootout, having it wouldn't make any difference
anyway—the end result would be Kailas's and my
deaths.

I reached the wall with seconds to spare. The gunfire
ceased. A few of the bolder guards approached the
smoldering ruins of my ride. Forcing myself through a
narrow gap in the barrier, I knelt, trying to catch my
breath. My hope now was that they'd send enough men
to investigate the strange attack to allow Kailas and I an
opportunity to steal a vehicle—preferably something
heavily armored—and blitz our way the hell out of
there. I withdrew the Glock from my belt. *Tight grip, tight
groups. Focus on the front sight. The first chance to dump your
handgun for a long gun, do it.* Long-archived bits of gun-
handling advice, picked up from gun shop owners I'd
interviewed to Army Rangers I'd overheard, came
racing to the front of my mind. Not that any of it
mattered. If confronted at all, I was screwed. A gunshot
inside the base would have hundreds of enemy infantry

swarming my ass before I could utter so much as an apologetic whimper.

I moved quietly between plywood-walled barracks, past a T-55 tank in the midst of having a track replaced, arcing my way toward a more permanent-looking stone edifice in the center of camp. I figured it was either an armory or a prison, and in either case, would have something in it I was looking for.

Voices. I flung open the nearest door and stuffed myself inside. The room was cramped, offensively humid. There was an offensive stench about it, too. I glanced behind me. In the dim light, I made out a row of large holes cut in a long wood bench, a pile of well-worn magazines piled to a side. I'd locked myself in the shitter.

Please, God, don't let me die ingloriously on the toilet, I thought, remembering my conversation with Kailas about the futility of prayer. I held my breath until the voices outside faded, then swung open the door and hauled ass around the corner. Watching behind me rather than looking where I was going, I smashed into a soldier's back. We both went down, my pistol tumbling into the dirt, his face and elbows skidding on the gravel.

"Cogar!" I looked up to see Kailas, hands bound, a relieved smile on his face.

I cursed as the soldier regained his feet, lifting his rifle to gun me down. I dove for his knees, dragging him to the ground. As we wrestled for his gun, I grunted, "Kailas, feel free to join in...if the mood...strikes you."

"What should I do? You want me to hit him?"

"No, no, you should just show him some pictures from your wallet—"

The guard landed a sharp left hook into my ribs, cutting me off. I traded him one to the chin.

"—or regale him with the riveting tale of your appendectomy," I continued, driving an elbow into my opponent's kidneys and grabbing for the barrel of his rifle. I pulled up sharply, slamming the soldier in the face with the front sight. He went limp, blood trickling down his forehead. I took a deep breath and wiped at the dust in my eyes.

"Thanks for your help, Kailas."

Eyeing the unconscious guard at his feet as he poked him with the toe of his shoe, Kailas asked, "What took you so long to get here?"

"I made the best time I could," I said, recovering my pistol. "Public transportation in this area is really erratic. Now, where can we find a ride? East or west?"

"West," he said, pointing east.

"You mean that way, then," I said, correcting him, pointing in the opposite direction.

"No, I'm sure my way is west. That's where they keep the vehicles."

"That may be where the vehicles are, but it isn't west—that's east. I just looked at a map, Kailas." My irritation was apparent, the urgency of the situation lost on my friend.

"But the sun—"

"Rises in the east!" I shouted, stabbing a hand at the dim ring of sunlight hovering behind a patchwork of mottled gray clouds overhead. Kailas was the sort of man who didn't get lost often, but only because he seldom went anywhere. He had always possessed a terrible sense of direction, and his stubborn insistence was not only misguided, in this moment, it was suicidal.

Staring at the sky, jaw slack, the far-away look in his eyes revealing his cogitation, Kailas said, "I'm beginning to see your point."

"Why don't you just humor me for a minute," I said, coaxing him forward.

We took no more than three steps before running into a squad of regime soldiers on their way back to their posts.

"See? I told you it was the other way," Kailas said as he dropped to his knees. I followed suit, dumping my pistol in the sand.

My arms were wrestled behind my back, a zip tie fastened around my wrists. A soldier with deep bags under his eyes and a shaved head glanced at the unconscious guard's body, then knelt before me, scooping the Glock from the ground. He tapped me on the nose with the muzzle and asked in heavily accented English, "Who are you?"

"Grant Cogar, civil engineer. I see a lot of potential with this place. I think if we were to add a few roundabouts and some potted plants, it'd be humming with tourists in no time."

"Why are you here?"

"Your mother gave me bad directions on my way out her bedroom window this morning." I turned and smirked at Kailas.

Our captor ignored my jab, reaching into his pocket with a free hand and withdrawing a cigarette. "You're with the rebels."

"What gave it away? Was it my Proud to Fight Assad embroidered uniform patch? Or the Free Syria tattoo on my left ass cheek?"

Kailas snickered. The soldier didn't find that funny.

"You are lucky we're not like your rebel friends, or we'd cut off your head with a dull knife the way they've done with our men. A firing squad will be more humane." The officer slipped the cigarette into his mouth but didn't light it. Probably waiting until after he'd killed us—like a relaxing post-coital smoke.

I sneered at him. "Glad to hear you guys have become so merciful. Sure makes all those dead civilians and all that irreplaceable historical architecture you incinerated seem like a distant memory."

"You think that's all our doing? We're trying to salvage what's left of our country, fighting against those who would see it shattered."

He had the faintest wisp of a valid point. Valid only because, on the off-chance the rebel forces did manage to unseat Assad, it wouldn't be all lilies and peace signs. At that very moment, while the FSA fought it out with Assad's forces, Sunni Islamic jihadists were rebuilding infrastructure in the north under their fundamentalist rule. It promised big trouble later, regardless of who won the war. More fighting and destruction would ensue as the country crumbled into a mosh pit of sectarian violence, assorted factions battling for control. Assad going down didn't mean peace; it just meant one less player in the game.

Worse, it wasn't as if winning really meant there was a clear victor: Everyone had already paid a heavy price to be part of this war, and I didn't see it coming to a neat conclusion in my lifetime.

I watched the soldier check the Glock's chamber, and then line the pistol up with my forehead.

He'd had enough talk.

Wincing as I looked down the pistol's dark bore, I asked, "What happened to the firing squad?"

"Why waste bullets? You only need one," he said.

"You can't know that for sure," I said, my voice urgent. "Why, I'll bet it'll take that entire magazine to kill me. Just think how tired your trigger finger will get doing all that work. It's an inefficient use of your time, and your supervisor will not be pleased. I suggest we convene a committee to decide the best course of action. I'll bring the coffee and donuts, you book the conference room. I'll just need you to untie me. We can meet back here in an hour."

The soldier took up the trigger's slack.

Kailas squirmed, jockeying until he blocked the pistol barrel with his chest.

"Kailas, no!" I cried.

The soldier planted his palm against Kailas's forehead and shoved him out of the way.

As I took what I suspected were my final breaths, I looked over my executioner's shoulder and spotted an ethereal figure approaching. A woman. But unlike the Kurdish fighters who had cast aside their femininity for the sake of practicality during the fighting, this woman wore a black, sleeveless dress and clutched an expensive-looking handbag. Her meticulously styled, chin-length brown hair swayed with her hips as she slowly approached. So out of place was her refined appearance and beauty, I momentarily considered that she must be my own angel of death—a representation of a forgotten lover come to take me to some new tier of hell.

She stopped before us. Guns were lowered, eyes downcast in deference. My executioner let his cigarette drop from his mouth.

"What's your name?" Her voice resonated with confidence and a subtle British accent.

"Grant Cogar, *Chicago Herald*. The man beside me is my trusty sidekick, Kailas Raahi. His tribe kicked him out for marrying an Apache squaw, and he's since become my footman. I hope you'll forgive my banality, but might I ask what such a beautiful woman is doing in a place like this?" My executioner grabbed hold of my hair and planted my face against the ground as if to punish me for speaking.

"Just going for a walk. Getting out of the house. It can be so dull just sitting around at home," she replied airily, as though she'd just bumped into us in the middle of an English garden. Removing a clamshell mirror from her purse, she swept her hair over her ear.

"I was thinking the same thing when the shelling started this morning. Dreadfully mundane," I said, my cheek grinding against a shard of concrete as the guard continued to hold me down.

She smiled faintly, without showing any teeth. "You Americans have a wonderful sense of humor."

I glanced sideways at my captor. "Compared to your countrymen, maybe."

"How brave you must be," she said, "to keep such humor even when your life is ending. Like a smiling paper man trapped in a rainstorm." Her eyes scanned Kailas and me. She waved a hand at the guard holding me down. "Release them."

I took a deep, relieved breath, and renewed my ingratiating efforts twofold.

"I apologize for my appearance, ma'am," I said as I extended my cuffed hands for a handshake. "Conditions are a bit unfavorable out here."

"You look a bit rugged, but I suspect you clean up nicely," she said, placing her fingertips into the palm of my hand and stepping toward me. "Perhaps you would be available to join me at my home? I could use the company."

"I'd be honored. But I don't know your name."

Before she could answer, the outpost's commanding officer—up to this point distracted by a conversation he'd been holding via push-to-talk radio—approached in the same rumbling fashion as a charging water buffalo, his broad head angled forward, face contorted in an ugly sort of pout.

"Sameera, what are you doing?" he asked, his voice more of a whine than the intimidating challenge I'd expected. "These men are with the rebels."

"No they're not, Colonel. They're American journalists. If you could keep your finger off your rifle's trigger long enough to ask a simple question, you'd know these things."

"Your husband may be a general, but that doesn't mean you carry the same influence. You have no business out here. I can handle my men without your interference."

"I don't doubt you're very adept at handling your men," she replied calmly. "I thought I'd save these men from such a fate."

It took the colonel a moment to comprehend her insinuation. When he did, he frowned and said, "Your husband will hear of your impudence, Sameera."

"We're not on a first-name basis, Colonel. I'd appreciate it if you'd refer to me only as Mrs. Sabbagh, and add a little civility to your tone. It won't kill you." She stepped toward him, her slender hands wrapped tightly around the strap of her purse. "But my husband might if you ever again intimate I'm not permitted to go where or do what I please."

The colonel stiffened, raising his chin before turning on a heel and marching back toward his men.

"Care to join me?" Sameera asked as she turned back to me, her tone instantly brightening as she waved a hand toward a waiting car in the distance.

"It would be our pleasure." I slipped my bound arms under my feet and stood. Joining the general's wife, I offered her my arm. Looking down at Kailas as he twisted in the dirt, battling his restraints in an effort to stand, I said, "Kailas, stay close. I don't need you wandering off again."

14
Riding Lesson

I spent the brief, silent drive looking out the window as the rubble, the shell craters, the general state of ruination, faded, transitioning to what I imagined the country had looked like before the fighting. We rolled through two checkpoints manned by dozens of sullen-looking regime soldiers before the driver of our Rolls Royce pulled up to a decorative gate mounted to a ten-foot-tall brick wall encircling the Sabbagh estate. The home loomed in the distance, partially hidden by flowering citrus trees. Tall Doric columns like those of the Greek Parthenon supported a grand triangular pediment at the building's front. Above it all, on the rooftop, appeared the silhouette of two soldiers—snipers on overwatch.

The place was gorgeous, carefully manicured and apparently untouched by the raging war.

I hated it.

"Such a beautiful day, isn't it?" Sameera asked, opening the door and stepping out of the car.

It had been a pretty shitty day, actually. I looked to Kailas and saw him open his mouth to echo my thoughts. I shook my head.

The estate's groom strode toward us, leading a trio of jet-black Hanoverian horses across the lawn.

"Do you know how to ride, gentlemen?" Sameera asked as the groom took a knee, offering his bent leg as a platform for her to mount the horse. She gracefully swung into place, sidesaddle, holding the reins firmly.

"Enough to get by," I said, approaching one of the horses and patting its nose before grabbing the reins in my left hand, planting my left foot in a stirrup, and swinging myself up. "A Pashtun family in Afghanistan taught me. They took me in for a while after I got separated from the infantry platoon I'd been following on night raids."

Though initially that family had only reluctantly protected me from the Taliban out of respect for their ethical code—the Pashtunwali—we became fast friends. I hadn't thought about them in some time. I hoped they were still alive. Years had passed. Tumultuous ones.

"I bet you don't miss those days of playing public relations specialist for the Army," Kailas said. He pulled a tuft of grass and let the blades flutter in the breeze. Even my mentor, who had been in the country for less than twenty-four hours, seemed to appreciate the surrounding verdure. "God knows, I haven't gotten a hard-hitting piece from Logan in years. Everything he writes comes off as a press release for the military."

I clicked my tongue and urged my mount forward, walking a large circle around the Rolls Royce. "That's because Logan is too passive for his own good. Did you know he once called me long-distance to apologize when one of his pieces bumped mine from the front page?" I chuckled. "I don't know. Embedded journalism is weird; it's like the morning after having drunken sex with a roommate. You're still stuck living together, you don't really know how to behave around one another, but you now have this uncomfortably intimate knowledge that can't be ignored. Are we friends? Are we lovers? Are you going to tell our mutual friends how I look naked?" My mount tested my competence by stretching his neck toward the grass underfoot. I rebuked him with a sharp tug on the reins. "By the time a reporter proves they aren't just a nuisance and they start getting some decent info, they've become so close to their unit, they can't stay objective. That's where Logan's at. I've been there; you depend on your guys to feed you, house you, and keep you alive when the enemy is shooting at you. Writing anything unflattering about them feels like betrayal. In

Logan's case, say he writes something the base commander or public relations department doesn't like. Then what? If you run it, the guys he works with will go out of their way to ensure he never leaves the FOB, or will make him wish he hadn't. But like you said, if he doesn't report the uncomfortable truth, is he really reporting at all? Should he just don a ball cap with Stars and Stripes on it and throw out any work that doesn't paint the military in the most flattering light?"

Kailas approached the third horse slowly. Then, apparently thinking better of it, he returned to the car, leaning against the trunk. "So why do it at all? I mean, you've gone solo for years in warzones, and you seem to produce mostly acceptable work."

"I do better than satisfactory work, Kailas, you enfeebled geriatric. I don't do the embedded thing anymore because I can get better stories on my own, and this way I don't feel like I'm constantly being babysat."

Sameera twirled a finger through her horse's mane, looking bored.

I nudged my mount alongside hers. "I'm sorry, Sameera. Kailas and I have a tendency to get lost talking shop sometimes. We can go now."

Kailas cleared his throat, staring at me as he bumped a nervous rhythm on the Rolls' trunk with his balled fist.

"What?" I asked.

He mumbled, "I don't ride. I don't...I don't do horses."

"Why the hell not?"

"I live in Chicago, and horses don't come with a steering wheel. Besides, they're unpredictable. And huge."

"You're more than welcome to ride in the car, Mr. Raahi," Sameera said pleasantly.

I could tell what he was thinking. After all he'd seen since arriving, Kailas didn't want to get separated from me again, even for a few minutes. He also didn't want to get on that horse. I watched, entertained, as he contemplated which of the two evils he'd choose.

He finally decided. "I'd be happy to walk the horse back to the stable, following you two."

"Whatever you'd like," Sameera said. She clicked her tongue, tapping her heels lightly against the horse's ribs. She took off at a slow trot, her body movement synchronized with the animal's even gait.

I followed, smiling at Kailas over my shoulder as he reluctantly approached the last horse as though it were a coiled cobra, hissing and prepared to strike. He grasped at the reins, the horse following obediently. But Kailas was skeptical. He kept his eyes on the animal as he walked.

"You're a natural, Mr. Cogar," Sameera said, looking over her shoulder at me as she coaxed her horse to a canter. "You'll have to give me my next riding lesson."

The double entendre wasn't lost on me. Suddenly, I could perfectly understand who I was dealing with. The sudden appearance of this elegant temptress, and her peculiar interest in me—a begrimed foreigner about to be put to death—had seemed bizarre even in my desperation. But now, standing in the cool shade of her imposing palace, basking in the aura of affluence that emanated from her with the same tantalizing intrigue as her perfume, it all became clear: Here was a woman suffering from an incurable boredom, looking for a project—a new pet. A stallion to ride.

I smiled, unabashedly admiring her shapely rear as she bounced up and down atop the saddle. The day was looking up.

15
Wink Wink Murder

That evening, after Sameera had spent the day giving us a slow tour of the estate while dispensing a steady regimen of shameless flirtation, we met in General Sabbagh's library for a meal. The walls were lined with leather-bound books—pristine, almost certainly unread. A towering oil-painted likeness of President Assad hung proudly against the fleur-de-lis wallpaper. The artist had casually reduced the elf-like prominence of the man's ears, but I took notice.

"I thought we'd enjoy a casual dinner in the study," Sameera said, gliding to a Victorian loveseat and gesturing for me to sit beside her. "Dining rooms are so cold and formal. I prefer an intimate setting, instead."

Reluctantly, Kailas eased himself into a wingback chair. He sat on the very edge of the cushion, the heel of his shoe scraping anxiously against the chair's ball-and-claw foot. I could tell the mangled state of his slacks bothered him, his hands always resting over the fresh tears in his knees.

Three settings had already been placed on a large walnut coffee table in the room's center. An elderly man with skin the texture of beef jerky stepped carefully into the room supporting a large silver platter. He wore a dusty tuxedo, and looked to be an original fixture of the mansion. His attire would certainly make his funeral preparations simpler; they wouldn't even need to change his clothes.

As he set the food before us, Sameera said a short prayer, ending it with, "*Allah, Sourya, Bashar, bas.*"

Unrolling my silverware and laying the cloth napkin over my knee, I said, "I've heard that before. What does it mean?"

"God, Syria, Bashar, and nothing more."

"At the risk of coming across as an unappreciative guest," Kailas said, abruptly dropping his silverware on his plate, "after seeing what your beloved Bashar has done to this country, I can't in good faith eat your food or enjoy your hospitality. Come on, Cogar, what are we doing here?"

I cleared my throat and glared at him. The dummy was going to get us executed. More importantly, I stood a very good chance of scoring with a beautiful woman for the first time in almost a year, and he was going to spoil it by his unwillingness to keep his trap shut.

"I think what my friend here means to say is, we appreciate your kindness, but find Assad's actions disagreeable from a humanitarian perspective," I said, trying to backpedal. The old man leaned over the table as he began pouring tea, ignoring me when I declined, filling my cup to the brim.

Still perfectly composed, Sameera said, "But Mr. Cogar, as an experienced journalist, I would think you of all people would understand the nature of war. No one escapes unscathed. Bashar is not an evil man as the world has portrayed him; he's doing what is necessary to keep his country from spiraling into chaos."

"If this isn't chaos, what the hell is it?" Kailas asked, leaning forward. There was the old Kailas. With all the tumult of the day, and the unusual reticence that had overcome my mentor since I'd found him, I'd briefly forgotten how bold and merciless he typically was. He thrived on debate, had made a living immersed in it. Angry readers, embittered advertisers, caviling writers and editors—he dealt with them every day. After so many years, I think he'd actually learned to enjoy the altercations and seek them out, much like an old soldier hanging around the bar at the VFW, bemoaning the absence of fights like the ones back in the good old days and challenging to a brawl anyone who came through the door.

Crossing her legs and returning her cup of tea to the table, Sameera spoke with measured elocution.

"This is Syria. It is my home, Mr. Raahi. I know you don't agree with what's happening here, but all of us, you included, are helpless to stop what's been set in motion."

Kailas grumbled, "At least some people are trying."

"How about we forego dinner and play a game?" I shouted, slapping my open palms against the table. The longer I let Kailas and Sameera talk, the more likely we were to go from honored guests to moving target practice for the estate's guards.

"What did you have in mind, Mr. Cogar?"

"How about a classic? Kailas, you remember the *Herald* Christmas parties? Back when we had the budget for a Christmas party? What was that game called that everyone loved so much?"

"Wink Wink Murder," he said. "It's an imbecilic game played by loud, drunk people. If you recall, the last time we played it, you ended the night by punching Justin in the nose."

"And tell me that wasn't the highlight of everyone's evening," I replied.

"How does one play this game?" Sameera asked, suddenly looking far more jovial, her smooth skin glowing in the dim lamplight.

"It's pretty easy," Kailas said, capitulating to his hunger and snatching a lamb kebab from his plate. "We draw from a hat to determine who will be the murderer in the group and who will be the detective. Then, we continue our conversation. When the murderer makes eye contact with someone in the group and winks, that person feigns death. The detective just has to determine who the murderer is before everyone is killed."

"We'll need more people to play, then," Sameera said, ringing a small bell the butler had placed alongside the food. The antediluvian man shuffled in.

"Baltasar, would you gather the others and bring them in, please? We're going to play a game."

Within a few minutes, the room had been filled with housekeepers, dog walkers, grooms, and groundskeepers. Everyone drew from a salad bowl filled with slips of folded paper.

I withdrew a piece and carefully unfolded it. I'd drawn the role of detective.

"So what now?" Sameera asked. "We simply talk to one another?"

"That's it," I said.

"Well, why don't you tell us a story of your exploits as a journalist, Mr. Cogar? That should be as fully entertaining as the game we're playing. Surely you've met some fascinating people in your travels," Sameera said, casting me an impeccable, if exhaustedly rehearsed, smile.

I sat back in my seat and crossed a leg over my knee. Sure, I'd met some interesting folks. But I'd learned early in life that those idols hoisted atop a pedestal by the huddling, unwashed masses are really no different than the rest of us. Even the most fascinating people in the world are plain and boring on some level. Somewhere, right now, there's a Hollywood starlet searching her local grocery store for a certain brand of bran cereal that she insists comes with more raisins in it. Somewhere, an astronaut is scratching his ass while mowing his lawn, and a poet laureate is peeing in the shower.

"You know what? I've got a great story," I said, leaning forward and rubbing my hands together. I was suddenly feeling a bit feisty. "It's a tale of a few men who deemed themselves great." I glanced at the painting of Assad. "I've personally been to each of their countries and have seen the result of their rule. The first was named Hosni Mubarak, an Egyptian. A hard-nosed military man who paved the way for extreme corruption in Egypt, building hidden detention facilities for political activists rather than feed his starving people."

The housekeeper—a portly battleship of a woman—slumped in her seat, feigning death. I continued, sweeping eye contact at each of the participants.

"Another was a man named Omar al-Bashir, from Sudan. A dictator like so many others, Bashir was complicit in ethnic cleansing and systematic rape, and embezzled billions in state funds while his countrymen went hungry."

The butler's head slumped to his chest. He played the role of a dead man better than anyone I'd seen. I was tempted to lean over and check for a pulse.

"The third: Mohammed Omar Mujahid, an Afghan. Supreme commander of the Taliban, he was a one-eyed monster credited with bringing about an era of public executions, the use of children as human shields in battle, poisoning the water at women's schools, and otherwise driving his country further into savage antiquity."

A groom dropped, followed by the dog walker. I shifted my gaze to Sameera, realizing she had drawn the murderer.

"So what do these men have in common?" I asked, taking a long sip of tea. Scenes from my past, bodies strewn on the ground and the cries of wounded and those left behind to mourn, and the painful helplessness they inspired, came racing back. Sweat ran down my neck. My hand tightened around the teacup in my lap until I was sure it would shatter. Sameera's insistence on Assad's innocence and the necessity of war was the exact reason Syria was lost. Because there were so many people like her who found it easier, less cognitively draining, to dismiss the whole lot as inevitable—like a sickness that just needed to run its course. Drink lots of fluids and get plenty of rest, and it will resolve itself. Only, it wouldn't. Hers was the blind eye that had given every violent bastard on all sides of the conflict the opportunity to turn this war into a disease with no cure.

I whispered, "They all turned their countries into sanguinary wastelands with their shared delusion of divine authority, and they did it with impunity. Not unlike your beloved president."

Sameera kept her eyes locked on mine. There was no anger there, no smolder. Cold. A calculated stare, the gears churning as she weighed my words. Then, slowly, she moved her stare to Kailas.

I stabbed a finger toward her and whispered, "Murderer."

16
Date Night

After half an hour spent with razor and soap shaving and chiseling away the strata of filth from myself in the shower—feeling a bit guilty about taking advantage of such a luxury when so many others didn't even have clean drinking water—I emerged to find a neatly pressed suit hanging from my guest room's open armoire, and a plate lined with crackers and caviar on the nightstand. Drying myself, I slipped the slacks on to find them a little shorter and looser around the middle than was comfortable.

It suddenly occurred to me that the outfit had likely come directly from General Sabbagh's closet. I felt dirtier putting the man's clothes on than I had with weeks of crusted sweat and mud embedded in my skin.

I stuffed a cracker into my mouth and suddenly realized how desperately hungry I was after having essentially skipped dinner. Someone knocked on the door. I stuffed another two crackers into a cheek and followed them with a caviar chaser.

"Mr. Cogar? Are you ready?" asked one of the servants from the hallway. I opened the door to find myself face-to-face with the crusty butler.

"Ready for what?" I said, crumbs falling down my shirt as I buttoned it up. I left my dirty clothes in a pile at the foot of the room's bed, but transferred my notes and wallet to the inside pocket of my suit jacket.

"Mrs. Sabbagh would like to see you. Please follow me."

The man led me down the hallway—the floor made up of large, flat stones such as those found in European castles and beer halls—and through a set of broad double doors with hand-forged iron hinges. Reaching the end of the hallway, my hoary friend bowed and left me, his polished shoes clicking on the stone as he vanished into the darkness. I tightened the knot on my tie, checking it in the reflection of the hallway mirror. I wrestled with it for a moment longer before deciding against wearing it entirely. Pulling a bouquet of fresh flowers from a vase displayed below the mirror, I slipped the tie over my head and stuffed it into the glass.

Turning toward the door, the tie, one end looped around the button on my suit jacket's sleeve and the other submerged in the green plant water at the bottom of the vase, slid the vessel to the edge of the table. It teetered for a second, and then fell and burst loudly on the stone floor. I winced, and then swept the glass shards under the hallway rug with the sole of my shoe, hoping Sameera hadn't heard me.

I grabbed the flowers and knocked lightly, opening the door to a sizeable bedroom illuminated by flickering candles, smelling of lavender perfume and fresh rose petals. They both seemed alien to me after having spent so much time with the smell of putrescence and death on the air.

"Mr. Cogar, I see you got my message."

I scanned Sameera's slender legs, toes to hips, as they emerged from a petite pink negligee. My eyes moved from her narrow waist to her small, firm breasts, rising and falling with each long breath. She twirled a finger around one of the thin spaghetti straps on her shoulder as she lay on the bed, her toffee-toned skin aglow in the candlelight. Frankly, after ten months spent sleeping on the steel bed of a truck, I was more interested in getting in the bed to sleep than to play. Sheets of burlap would have felt like gossamer had I just been laying on that mattress.

"I think I've gotten the message very clearly," I said, gently placing the bundle of flowers I carried atop her dresser.

She moved from the mattress, letting her shoulder straps slide down her upper arms. The fabric of her negligee clung to her skin, but only just. "Can I get you a drink?" she asked.

"I'm trying to quit. Besides, how would your husband feel about a guest like myself enjoying his liquor with his beautiful, but undeniably scantily clad wife?"

"You could add lonely to that description, too, Mr. Cogar," she said, tossing her hair and looking at me over her shoulder as she ran her fingers up the neck of the bottle.

"You can call me Grant."

"All right, Grant. You see, my husband's one of those types who lives for war. He finally has a good one to play in. One where he can do more than just order his men to march around like toy soldiers." She unraveled the foil around the bottle's cork and lifted the wire cage. "Bassem hasn't given me so much as a thought since this began two years ago, and hasn't been home in as long." The bottle popped loudly. Sameera flicked the cork into the room's corner and began pouring the bubbly into a crystal flute.

"I see." I softly touched her arm with the tips of my fingers. I was lonely, too. I hadn't experienced a ten-month dry spell since I was sixteen. Such a drought is like a decade to a man with a normal libido.

Sameera continued, "Not that it would matter. He married me because he needed an attractive showpiece to grace his arm during parades—a woman of comparable charm and beauty to the good president Assad's wife, Asma."

She spat the last word as though it tasted bitter.

"So you would call this a loveless marriage?" I asked.

"I think that would be fair to say," she replied. Running her fingers along my jaw, she tousled my hair. "You clean up nicely."

"Yeah? Maybe I should give up on this newspaper business. You think I could make it in television?"

"Oh, certainly," she said, leaning against the wall and sliding her bare leg up the seam of my trousers, my pants getting shorter by the second.

"I'm beginning to think I need to be taken captive more often," I said.

She smiled seductively after taking a long drink of champagne. Then, setting her glass down, she stepped close to me and ran her hands beneath my shirt. They were cold.

"As my prisoner, I order you to make love to me."

Our coupling was intense. Her hunger rivaled my own, her unbridled moans crescendoing to screams in Arabic that needed no translation. When we'd climaxed for the second time, her back-scratching supplications loud enough to be heard throughout the building, we laid back, naked and sweat-soaked. Sameera rolled to her side, smiled and sighed softly, eyes closed, and immediately fell asleep. She looked peaceful, sweet.

I had to leave.

I would gladly make love to a lonely woman, even a married one if the husband's character warranted the infidelity—and a violent Syrian dictator's golf buddy definitely met the criteria—but dozing in her marital bed after wearing her husband's clothes was too unpalatable, even for me.

I began pulling my pants on, careful not to wake her. That's when I caught my reflection in her dresser mirror. It was the first time I'd seen myself naked in months. I'd become emaciated, gaunt. The faint outline of ribs and hipbones pushed against my skin. Old, recognizable wounds had been rendered unfamiliar, deformed as the skin stretched, pulled taught. That one, a thick white scar on my collarbone, had been left behind when a Ranger medic had fished out a piece of Iraqi shrapnel from my skin. The rough, rose-colored patch on my calf came from a Palestinian flash-bang grenade that had exploded at my feet. A patchwork of stab wounds and full-moon bullet holes filled out the space in between.

I turned away, ashamed. What had I become? I looked a step removed from the starving Sudanese kids I used to give my camp dinners to. I seldom slept more than a few hours each night whether as a result of artillery shells or night terrors, and more importantly, I'd lost what little sense of purpose I'd had when I'd started out as a reporter. Unlike the people who had stayed because this was their country, I'd stayed only because there was nothing for me anywhere else. But I was beginning to realize: Staying here was killing me. It was killing me, and I desperately wanted to live.

Shuffling my shirt on and quietly opening the door to the hallway, I rushed toward my room. I needed another shower. As I turned the corner, I spotted the dark outline of a figure peeking out of a doorway.

"What are you doing up?" Kailas asked.

"Same could be asked of you."

After a moment of silence spent contemplating an answer, he said, "I needed to take a piss."

"Yeah. Same."

We both stood there, not speaking, a mutual understanding that neither of us was really looking for the bathroom.

Kailas cleared his throat. "That, and I can't sleep worth shit away from home. Besides, there's something I don't trust about this woman, this place, this fucking country."

"I know the feeling," I said, joining him. "I don't know about you, but I'd kinda like to see what else is going on here. The whole 'perfectly groomed mansion in the middle of a warzone' seems oddly reminiscent of Himmler's castle to me."

We set out down the hallway, shuffling our way through winding corridors lined with tapestries and medieval furniture. Kailas cleared his throat.

"I've been meaning to talk to you about something, Cogar."

"Thanks, Dad, but I've already gotten the birds-and-bees talk. Actually, from the same girl who took my virginity. I learned plenty that day. It was a lot for a fourteen-year-old to absorb."

"Not that, you sick fucker." He paused, weighing his words carefully. "At the last board of directors meeting, I was told in no uncertain terms that I needed to cut our expenses to make budget. They seemed to agree that the best way to do that was to scale back our foreign coverage." He glanced at me to see if I had grasped where he was heading. I ignored him. If he was going to fire me, I wanted him to have to work for it.

He continued, "I let Logan go last week, and it's looking like, at least in the near future, I won't even have the budget to keep you on as a stringer. I might be able to send you out occasionally, or buy pieces you write on your own, but nothing to the scale you've done in the past."

I nodded without breaking pace. "It was just a matter of time. Don't feel bad about it, Kailas." The picture was becoming clearer. Kailas had come to Syria not to rescue me from capture, but because he saw me, and apparently my career, hurtling down a tunnel ending abruptly in a brick wall, and he felt partially responsible. His coming to Syria was less about bringing me home, and more a man desperately trying to reassemble the broken pieces of a friend's life. He didn't know how to do it, but damn it, he was up there swinging.

"What would you do differently if you were in my shoes?" he asked earnestly. "I feel like there must be some way to bring things back around."

"If you were really committed to saving the *Herald*, you'd start trafficking cocaine like that DeLorean guy back in the '80s. The love ain't real unless you're willing to face prison time."

"Be serious, Cogar."

"Fine. But in my defense, you've asked me that same question, rhetorically, for ten years. And if you were serious about asking my opinion, I might give you a serious answer." I reached out and tapped the frame of a particularly egregious attempt at an oil painting—a boy with a lopsided face holding a cartoonish lollipop— swinging it slightly askew, and continued on to the next in line.

"Okay, I'm serious. How would you battle a dying industry to make us profitable again? They're talking about putting in a paywall for our digital content. That might work."

I shook my head as I scooped up a handful of chocolate candies sitting in a crystal dish on one of the hall tables, popping a few into my mouth. Stale. "Good luck with that. People will just get their news somewhere else. Social media. Blogs. Their great uncle Tamir whose buddies at the coffee shop still have connections to the home country."

"But that's unvetted information. They wouldn't know if it was true."

"How is that different from news coverage by major media networks these days? They don't even apologize when they get it wrong anymore, since they're perpetually running misinformation and people have proven they'll keep watching. It's all bullshit. You know why you guys aren't profitable? Because people don't actually want to know what's happening. That's where you and the board of directors are getting it wrong. Readers don't want hard facts, even if they say they do. They want sensationalist drivel. Something that gets them pissed off or aroused. They don't want news; they want entertainment, stimulation. That's why I'll die penniless and unknown while every right-wing conspiracy theorist radio host and liberal talking head make a killing." I bumped another painting.

"It's not that bad."

"Well it sure as hell isn't good. You want to stick with the honest approach? The best thing you could do is to get away from cursory news blurbs, the same shit you can find on the Internet for free, and start doing some deep dives. Features that read like essays. Charge for that. Find the few people out there who are willing to pay for knowledge, not just the sports scores, but a deeper, more comprehensive understanding of an issue. Then, you send guys like me into the shit for six months and have us write a 50,000-word piece. See where that lands."

"I'd have more luck trying to convince the board of directors to go the drug-selling route," Kailas said. "You're a romantic."

"You're just figuring this out? How many times did you walk in on me and my girlfriends back in high school?" I went to bump another painting, struck it too hard, and it fell to the floor. I quickly returned it to its place on the wall and took a step away. Thinking better of it, I returned and carefully tweaked it out of square like I'd done to the rest.

"Not like that. You really see yourself as some kind of Edward R. Murrow figure, don't you? The last bastion of honest reporting and government watchdoggery."

"You're scoffing," I said.

"I'm not, I'm really not." Kailas said, jangling the loose change in his pocket. "But come on. No wonder you're always getting invited to give lectures at university J-schools; even with the whole 'hardened war correspondent' image you try so hard to maintain, you're an idealist, aren't you?"

"I'm an incurable realist, Kailas. And for your information, I've not been invited back to speak at any universities since security escorted me out of DePauw."

"DePauw is in Indiana," Kailas corrected. "You were at DePaul."

"Well it started with a D, wherever it was. And to your point about Murrow, you know how I feel about broadcast. No, I've always seen myself as more of an Ernie-Pyle-type with a touch of Hunter S.'s salty language, a dash of Papa Hemingway's chest hair, and a healthy portion of Casanova's womanizing."

"Casanova wasn't a journalist."

"Well he was at least a quarter of the way there," I said.

We reached the end of the hallway and started down a narrow concrete stairway leading to the basement.

"Maybe you should come with me to the next meeting and tell the board what you told me," Kailas said, taking each step carefully. "They might listen."

I chuckled. "No thanks. Every time I offer my suggestions to one of those guys in suits, they give me this look as though I've just broken routine at the nursing home."

"All joking aside, I'm really sorry, Cogar," Kailas said. His voice betrayed his solemnity. "You know if there were any other way to keep you working for the *Herald*, I'd find it. It eats me up that I can't."

I slowed my steps, eventually turning to look at him. There was something that had been bothering me since we arrived, and now was as good a time as any to bring it up.

"Back at the outpost. You tried to shield me from that soldier when he was ready to shoot me. You were going to take that bullet for me, weren't you?"

He cocked his head. "Why do you sound surprised?"

"Because," I swallowed hard, willing a sarcastic quip to present itself, some clever way to downplay the emotions pinballing inside my chest. Finding none, I blurted, "You just...you shouldn't have done that. You've got a family to go home to."

"So do you, kid."

Neither of us could look the other in the eye. He'd spoken the unspoken, the sentiment that neither of us had ever articulated despite our long history. We'd always had a grudging fondness for each other, but to hear him admit it, let alone suggest that I was part of his family, was startling in its sincerity.

I broke the silence. "I would hug you, but if anyone found out, I'd lose all my cred with my homies up in the Cook County pen." I extended my hand to him and he gave it a firm shake.

Smirking, he said, "A man's reputation is everything."

As we continued on, eventually reaching the bottom of the stairway, I leaned into the first room in the narrow tunnel and flipped a light switch. The walls were covered in hundreds of framed football jerseys, autographed balls, and sports memorabilia.

"See Kailas? Even Syrian generals are only interested in sports scores. Give up on the news, already, and entertain me, goddammit."

The basement began to take on a look disparate to the old-money feel of the rest of the estate. The doors aboveground had been made of ornately crafted hardwoods, framed in hand-carved molding. Those in the basement were Cold War relics made of riveted steel turned rusty from the subterranean humidity.

"We should probably get back to our rooms, Cogar," Kailas said as he suppressed a shiver. "I don't like the looks of this place. Kinda worried we're going to stumble upon a bunch of people strung up in chains."

"Well if we did, they would need our help. We owe it to them to continue on." I poked my head into another room and flipped the lights on. "Hey, check this out. It may not be a dungeon, but I have a feeling the good general would probably be just as upset that we found it. Looks like a control room of some sort."

Sleeping LCD monitors spanned the concrete walls. LED lights flooded the room in an eerie paleness, revealing a large safe sitting in a corner, bolted to the floor.

"Cogar, don't. We shouldn't even be here," Kailas said.

"Why not? We're guests, are we not? Hell, I'm still just looking for a place to take a piss, if anyone asks." Running my hand over the digital keypad on the safe door's front, I mused, "What do you suppose ol' Bassem made his passcode? *Sameera…*" I said, pressing the numbers corresponding to the letters of her name. The lock beeped with each push, and then blinked red. I tried the latch. Locked.

"Figures. How could he even wonder why his wife would sleep with me?"

"You slept with her already?" Kailas asked. "Christ, you meet a woman while looking like something my cat would leave on my front doorstep, but still, within twelve hours, you've already gotten her clothes off. It defies logic."

"When have you ever known me to waste time in getting to know a beautiful woman?"

"Even when that beautiful woman is complicit in genocide?"

"We can't know that for certain," I said.

"Well one thing is certain: It's a curiosity why she'd settle for you."

"She's heard the other girls talk."

"And she didn't laugh you out of her bedroom?" Kailas snickered—a throaty, devious laugh he'd perfected over years of tormenting hapless staff writers.

"I have never once been laughed out of a bedroom," I argued. "Chased out at gunpoint, yes. But never laughed out."

Kailas refused to enter the room, staring down the hallway as he hovered near the door. I resumed my efforts to break into the general's safe.

"I guess we'll have to try the old standbys. We'll see how clever this fella is."

"Cogar, I really don't think this is wise."

Ignoring him, I continued. "How about *password*."

The lock blinked red again, and the latch wouldn't budge.

"Cogar, that thing's gotta have a lockout mechanism. You've already used two tries. What if it notifies this guy after the third?"

"Okay, okay. I'll stop after this last one, okay?" I punched zero six times. The light blinked green, and the locking bolts clicked open. I grinned stupidly at my mentor. "See? The world isn't really so big and wild, Kailas. A Syrian warlord has the same password that half the population of the United States uses for their ATM and computer passwords."

Swinging open the door, my grin disappeared. Kailas's curiosity got the better of him, and he drifted into the room, looking over my shoulder at the safe's contents.

"Well that's not what I expected to find in here," I said, leaning inside, hovering above a small aluminum briefcase. The safe was empty, otherwise. "How much cash or gold could he possibly have in a box this small?"

"Um, Cogar? The symbol." Kailas pointed at the radioactive emblem adhered to the case's lid and shrunk back into the hallway.

"Yeah, I had a sticker just like that I kept on my box of porno magazines as a teenager. Or was it Mister Ick?"

The black LCD monitors cast a sudden glow as they came awake behind us.

Sameera's face filled the screen. She smiled curtly as she wiped at her face with a cotton ball, dark eyeliner bleeding into the white. The makeup had hidden her age.

"Grant, Mr. Raahi, I must protest you searching through my husband's things in such a fashion. Hardly the behavior of good houseguests."

"Our sincere apologies," I said loudly and with forced enthusiasm as I scooted away from the safe. "Just looking for the toilet, actually. Got a little off-course, that's all."

Booted footsteps echoed along the concrete corridor outside the room. Two guards, AKM rifles in hand, burst through the door, weapons raised.

Sameera, gathering her dark hair into a ponytail, stood up, her face shrinking in the monitors, and said, "Oh, my poor little paper man. You've disappointed me. You've ventured into a world in which you don't belong. Now the storm clouds have gathered, and you've no place to run."

17
Puppies and Giggles

We stepped down the rust-coated spiral stairway of a flooded missile silo beneath the Sabbagh estate. The damp air, the heavy shadows, and the derelict, industrial look of the place gave me a chill, but nothing like the gnawing discomfort I felt knowing what was about to happen next.

"At least there's no water for me to drown in out here in the desert," I said sarcastically. "It should be perfectly safe and dry, right?"

One of Sameera's guards prodded me in the spine with the muzzle of his rifle as I hesitated, staring over the edge of the chasm. Below, the suspension rods and coil springs of the silo's shock mounts poked out of the algae-covered water.

"You still can't swim?" Kailas asked.

"Can't is an ugly word. Perform poorly might be more appropriate. Envision a stumpy-legged bulldog trying to stay afloat, only with less natural buoyancy and more aimless splashing."

Peering over the edge, Kailas said, "I can't shake the feeling that they've got something unpleasant planned for us, Cogar. And what's especially curious is, I also can't help but to feel as though this is all your fault." His voice echoed in the cavernous space.

"My fault? How do you figure? Life was all puppies and giggles until you showed up."

"You weren't content enjoying the hospitality of a beautiful woman," he said with a false smile, looking ingenuously over his shoulder at Sameera as she stepped daintily down the stairway behind us. She smiled graciously at him but made no effort to stop the guards from pushing us forward. "You just had to go poking around."

"I'm curious by nature," I replied. "We keep moving forward, opening new doors and doing new things, because we're curious. Walt Disney said that."

"Walt Disney was an anti-Semitic Nazi."

"Yes, but the man had a great mustache. Anyway, you're blaming me for being a good investigative reporter while ignoring the fact that Sameera there, beautiful as she is—" I looked over my shoulder and flashed a broad, exaggerated smile at her,"—is assisting her husband in his plot to kill his buddy, President Assad."

Kailas shook his head. "That's a completely unsubstantiated…wait, why would that be a bad thing?"

"Because the polonium—I'm assuming that's what was in the little shiny case upstairs—is the same dirty little radioactive isotope used to kill Yasser Arafat."

"So?" Kailas said, stopping and refusing to move forward even as the guard behind him pushed his shoulder. "Isn't killing Assad the whole point behind this war? They'd be doing you a favor."

I sighed and turned around to face my mentor, the guard standing before me bearing a look of disdain and impatience matching my own. The two soldiers were undoubtedly displeased that they'd been roused from their beds to come deal with us, and were likely in a hurry to do the deed and get back to sleep.

"The Israelis killed Arafat."

"Allegedly," Kailas corrected.

"Oh, they killed him. Dropped a speck of that polonium in his cornflakes. Now, if someone in Assad's inner circle were to use the same stuff on him, it could be used to point a big fat finger at the Israelis. General Sabbagh would be the first to step up to assume the presidency following Assad's untimely death—that's what he stands to gain—and would use his buddy's assassination as leverage to convince the Iranians to send more of their Qods Force soldiers here to offset

Israel's ostensible meddling. Hezbollah would probably want a piece of that action, too. That'd help turn the tide of the war, hammering the final nail in the rebellion's coffin. Which, not coincidentally, would make now-President Sabbagh a very powerful man, indeed." I found myself buzzing with excitement as I narrated my hypothesis. "And you," I continued, pointing at Sameera as she stepped close, "You love this plan. Your husband becomes president; you become first lady. Replacing Asma would be a real pleasure for you, wouldn't it? You'd be on the world's stage—the striking, deadly Sameera, wife of the man who brought about the end of the bloodiest war of the century with an iron fist. So much more than Asma ever was or could have been."

"You certainly are a storyteller," Sameera replied, her mellifluous voice retaining its seductiveness even in insult. "Whether any of your story is true or not will just have to remain a mystery to you for the five minutes you've left to live," she whispered, running her hand along my cheek.

"But I thought we really had a connection," I said unenthusiastically as the guards pushed Kailas and me toward the stairway landing overlooking the edge of the pit. I glanced down at General Sabbagh's loafers on my feet, the toes sticking out from the edge of the concrete lip. I gripped the steel guardrails as the soldiers pushed me closer to the edge.

Sameera smiled disingenuously, "Grant, it wasn't even that good. A disappointment, really."

I looked over my shoulder, shocked. "Lady, that's just hurtful. It's one thing to execute a guy, but to insult his sexual prowess in front of his buddy? That's malicious."

She nodded to the guard holding his gun to my back. Before he could shove me off the edge and into the sludge hundreds of feet below, I jumped. Leaping toward the abyss, I grabbed at a winch chain suspended from the silo's retractable roof, my fingers slipping inside the wide links. My legs swung up as I crossed the expanse. I glanced back. One of the two guards—a short fellow, I suddenly noticed—opened fire. The rifle spat orange, the muzzle rising as its bolt chattered and brass shell casings danced off the landing, plunging into the water below. Amidst the deafening echoes of the rifle's reports, I felt the slugs zip beneath my feet, slap the silo wall, and ricochet back against me in stinging fragments. The second guard shoved Kailas to the floor and stepped beside his friend, firing at me as my feet touched the far side of the silo. Pushing away from the wall at a perpendicular angle, I watched as the second guard's muzzle, mere inches from his partner's ear, barked loudly. The shattering report drove the shorter guard to his knees, the injured man clutching his ear and letting his rifle tip over the edge.

My momentum swung me back around, headed in a sweeping arc towards my captors and what I could only assume would be my certain death. I pulled my knees to my chest and held on tightly as I swung before the guard's line of fire.

That's when I heard the most welcome sound of any that exists on a battlefield—the *clink* of a rifle's bolt hanging back followed by beautiful, ringing silence.

The look on that guard's face as I neared him has stuck with me to this day. It wasn't panic or fear, but one of utter bewilderment. My foot struck him in the cheek, and he toppled forward, falling into the water below.

Taking my damn shoe with him.

Letting go of the chain, I fell hard on my tailbone beside the shorter guard, still cradling his ear and moaning.

"Shoots at me, takes my shoe...." I muttered, planting my foot against the injured guard's armpit and kicking. The man twisted as he toppled over the edge, striking the water below with a delayed slap.

Pulling myself to my feet, I reached down, removed my remaining shoe, and tossed it over the edge.

"Sameera, we need to talk," I said, extending my hands toward her. For a woman who seemed never at a loss for words, her mouth hung agape, her eyes reflecting panic as she backpedaled up the stairway. "We had a lovely time, didn't we? But I'm afraid my good friend and I..." I kicked my still-cowering editor with my socked foot. "...must be off. We'll always have last night, though," I said, wrapping her in my arms and kissing her passionately. Twirling us around slowly, I walked her toward the precipice edge and, smiling, planted my pointer finger on her collarbone. With the gentlest nudge, I sent her tumbling into the pit.

As she splashed down, I shouted, "I save my best lovemaking for women I actually like, by the way."

As I turned and began walking up the stairwell, Kailas said, "Cogar, wait. Shouldn't we…you know…give them something to hold onto? We can't just let them die."

I sighed. He was right. They would probably drown down there if we didn't do something. I'm many things, but a cold-blooded killer, I'm not.

I looked around until I found a release lever for the winch I'd been swinging on. Lifting the lever, I listened as the chain rolled down and broke the water's surface beside Sameera and her guards. It'd give them something to hold onto until someone came to extract them. Of course, they'd smell worse than the inside of a Porta-John at a chili cook-off by then.

Kailas, stepping up behind me and staring down at the three bodies treading water below, asked, "You do this sort of thing often?"

I wiggled my toes and sighed. "More often than I'd like."

18
Polonium

Making our way up the stairwell, I paused at the entrance to General Sabbagh's safe room. The lights had been left on, the television monitors still showing the bare wall of Sameera's bedroom.

"We can't leave that polonium, Kailas."

"Oh, we most certainly can," he said, stabbing the air in front of my face with his hand. "I'm done meddling in this country's affairs. I came here to get you, you utterly insane, totally heedless, unappreciative bastard. I found you, now I want to go home—and you're coming with me. End of fucking story."

I ignored him and dodged into the room, reopened the safe door, and tugged the case from within.

"See, Kailas?" I said, shaking the case at him. "Took two seconds. After all these years, you seem to think you can still coerce me into listening to your overcautious—"

The scream of the estate's alarms made me freeze mid sentence. I pinched my eyes closed, chagrined. The case must have been resting on some sort of pressure switch wired to the alarm system.

"I'm going to spend hours—no, days—berating you for what you just did, Cogar," Kailas yelled, rubbing the silver hair at his temples. "Later, when the threat of death isn't so…imminent."

Kailas and I sprinted up the steps, following the winding stone passageway as we looked for an exit—the unnerving shriek of the alarms echoing against the walls.

"There, Cogar. Door up ahead on the left," Kailas shouted.

Pushing through an arched, solid oak door that looked as though it'd been misappropriated from a mosque or temple, Kailas and I found ourselves in the Sabbagh Estate motor pool, the capacious room illuminated by moonlight streaming through the windows.

And this much was immediately clear: The naughty general had excellent taste.

I stepped past an onyx-colored Morgan Aeromax Coupé—the very sight of which gave me a tingly sensation below my belt—to a 1960s Bentley S2 parked nearby. Touching a hand to the grandiose chrome grill, I wrapped my fingers around the flying B hood ornament.

"Not the time, Cogar. Check for keys. We need to get out of here," Kailas said, panicking as he flung open the driver-side door of a Porsche 911 and slapped a hand on the steering column.

I nodded and gave the hood ornament a firm twist, snapping it off.

"Just a souvenir."

Kailas whimpered, "Cogar, I'm not finding any keys."

Booted footfalls sounded from the motor pool entrance. Someone barked an order.

Quickly scanning the garage as the first of the palace guard's bullets cracked over my head, my eyes settled on a monstrosity of a vehicle tucked in a dark corner. It looked like a moonshine-fueled invention of a band of anarchist hillbillies—a pickup truck or van that had been converted to an armored car. Undoubtedly a captured rebel innovation. The regime would never bother constructing such a macabre contraption—the Russians were far too eager to donate their gently used, mothball-and-Cosmoline-scented military surplus to Assad's cause.

Rusted steel plates, clumsily welded onto the frame in layers, gave the vehicle the appearance of a prehistoric, scaled monster. If nothing else, it would give us a place to hide from the guard's small arms fire until we could figure out a better solution. Gesturing to Kailas, I dashed toward the armored car, scrambled up its side, and flung open the top hatch. I dropped inside as a bullet ricocheted off the armor below and shattered the Porsche's windshield.

"Hey, it's roomy in here. And they've got TV!" I shouted giddily as I spotted three flat-screen monitors mounted at eye level where the windshield once was. Kailas slid headfirst through the aperture, crashed to the floor, then scrambled to his feet and yanked the hatch closed behind him, locking it.

"I don't care about the television, Cogar, tell me it has a key."

We ignored the muted *thunk* of jacketed lead slapping the car's thick steel shell as we searched for the ignition.

"Found it, thank God," Kailas panted, turning the key. The armored car coughed and shook as it started. "All right. Wait, where's the gas pedal? The brake? What the hell?" he said, patting the bare floor blindly with his palms.

Then, it dawned on me.

"Kailas, whoever built this thing deserves a goddamn engineering excellence award. Turn on the TV monitors and hold this." I unrolled a videogame controller from beneath the dashboard and handed it to Kailas.

"What am I supposed to do with this?" he asked, staring at the device as though it had fallen from the sky.

"Drive the car."

"No way."

"Right? How pointlessly clever is that?"

"Needlessly complicated. You know how to use one of these things?" Kailas asked, shaking the controller.

I shook my head as if someone had asked me to hold their pet snake. "No clue. Never owned one. You must have some experience with them, though. You've got kids."

"Do I look like my fucking kids, Cogar?" Kailas shouted, turning on the forward monitors. A set of sweeping carriage house doors, closed, popped up on the center monitor. The two side monitors completed a panoramic view of the motor pool's interior. More guards had arrived and were approaching our vehicle cautiously, rifles up.

The armored car's designer had used a security system's cameras to provide sight for steering without exposing the vehicle's passengers. It was just crazy enough to work.

"Hey, no need to get testy," I said, feeling our vehicle rock as the guards leapt aboard and worked to loosen the hatch. "But you're going to have a better chance than I am. I've still got your old TV you gave me when I graduated high school, and I still haven't figured out how to use the VCR properly."

"Odds or evens?" he said. "Come on, Cogar, it's only fair. Loser has to figure out how to drive this thing."

"Aren't things a little, I don't know, urgent for playing games?" I asked as one of the soldiers outside shoved what I assumed was a pry bar against the hatch cover overhead.

Kailas's face was stone. He wasn't budging.

"Fine. Evens."

I threw out a three, and Kailas pointed a single finger.

I roared triumphantly, "Every fucking time. Well Jeeves, drive us out of here, and don't spare the horses."

Kailas cursed under his breath, grabbed the controller, and pressed a button. One of the cameras swiveled.

Frustrated, Kailas let the controller drop. "See? I don't know how to do this, Cogar."

"Just press buttons until something happens," I said, inspecting the latch separating us from the soldiers outside. It was beginning to give, the hinge deforming under the pressure. "But hurry up."

Kailas began pressing every button on the controller. The vehicle suddenly lurched forward in a cloud of black exhaust, dumping our attackers off the roof as we crashed through the doors, shedding splintered wood and bits of glass as we sped through the estate's front lawn.

19
Hinds Close Behind

Kailas shook visibly, struggling to keep our vehicle on the asphalt.

"You all right, buddy?" I asked, patting him on the shoulder reassuringly.

"Just a little shaken up. This whole getting-shot-at thing doesn't agree with me." Even his voice—typically gruff and bold—quavered slightly over the hum of the armored car's engine.

"I've yet to meet anyone who it does agree with. You're dealing with the adrenaline dump right now. It'll pass. Hey, just imagine the stories you'll have when you get home, eh?"

My attempt at levity fell on deaf ears. Kailas was dumbfounded and terrified, just as I would have been if this had happened to me a decade ago, when I'd first started out. My nerves had grown a bit calloused with my prolonged exposure to the ragged edge, though. A day like today, marked by numerous near-death encounters, I now merely called Wednesday and relegated to my memory with the same degree of importance as any of those I spent in the *Herald's* offices or sorting through mail in my underwear at home.

I cleared my throat and said, "Well, we're out of the scary part of the journey, anyway. It'll be smooth sailing 'till Turkey."

On our left monitor, the azure waters of Al Assad Lake glistened pleasantly in the dying moonlight. A narrow band of glowing amber slipped over the horizon as the sun prepared to emerge. Maybe today wouldn't turn out to be so bad, I thought, breathing deeply and leaning my head against the armored car's rattling side. After all, I'd gotten a shower, I'd gotten laid, and I'd thrown a wrench in General Sabbagh's plans.

"Cogar, I've got bad news," Kailas exclaimed suddenly.

I looked up in a panic at the monitors expecting to see a roadblock in the distance or an enemy tank approaching.

"I forgot to tell you that you've been evicted from your apartment." He glanced at me over his shoulder with the ashamed, regretful look of someone who'd door-dinged a Ferrari.

"What made you think that this was the right time to tell me that?" I asked incredulously.

"I don't know. In case we die before we get back."

I shook my head, puzzled at his sense of priority.

"Somehow an eviction pales in comparison to our recent near-misses," I said. Anyway, I wasn't worried. My Bosnian landlord, Hasan, despite his money-centric nature, seemed to like having me around. He threatened to evict me all the time. It hadn't happened yet.

The armored car began to make a new noise. A steady thumping.

"You hear that?" I asked.

"Hear what?" Kailas asked, craning his head to listen. "Wait, that's not us, is it?"

A roaring detonation erupted on our right side. The open desert sands on the right monitor disappeared as the camera linked to it shattered. The entire vehicle rocked dangerously from the impact, tires chirping on the pavement as the blast lifted the car's back end.

"The fuck was that?" Kailas shouted as he attempted to right the car.

Flipping open one of the narrow shooting ports, I scanned the outside of the car. I didn't like what I saw.

"Kailas, I've got bad news."

He didn't bother asking what the news was. He'd already figured it out.

The thumping wasn't coming from our car; it was the rotothrob of one of Assad's Mi-24 helicopters. That boom had been an unguided rocket that had nearly vaporized us.

"I suppose we should feel flattered that they'd bother," I said, scrambling toward Kailas and gesturing wildly at a gravel offshoot off the main roadway. In the distance, rising from the lake's waters, stood a crumbling stone edifice, a ring of bastions protruding from it like the teeth of a gear.

Qal'at Ja'bar. A 7th century hilltop castle, and our Alamo.

"Kailas, see the citadel? The causeway leading to it? Go there. Do some bobbing and weaving, but head there."

"Shouldn't we stick to the road? The gravel will slow us down."

"Not enough to matter. Just do as I said."

"We'll be trapped in there. A dirt castle isn't going to protect us."

"You see anywhere else to hide? We're in the middle of a fucking desert, and I'm fresh out of brilliant plans. This one seems like the best of the worst right now, okay? Castle. Now."

Standing on the brakes, the tires squealing in protest as the armored car slid to a slow stop, Kailas began moving us in reverse. A parallel trail of impacting autocannon rounds tore up the earth on either side of our vehicle as the Hind flew by, carving a wide arc in the air, sweeping back around to face us.

"What the hell are you doing? I said drive toward the castle."

"Giving them the slip; evading like they do in the movies." Kailas flinched, scrunching his shoulders as one of the Hinds' rounds punched through our vehicle's roof and through the floorboards between us, leaving behind a narrow beam of moonlight.

I lunged forward, grabbing a handful of Kailas's shirt, and yelled in his ear, "It's never like they show it in action movies. Never ever. It's a motherfucking helicopter. You're not going to outmaneuver it. Just get us to cover and let's get off this rolling target, okay?"

"All right, all right," he said, planting his finger on the forward accelerator button. I tumbled backwards again, colliding with a large steel panel at the back of the car. Grabbing at its handle to keep my brains from being scrambled on the next jolt, I felt the panel give way. The steel door hinged open, revealing a small arsenal of rocket-propelled grenades. Ripping an RPG-7 rocket-propelled grenade launcher from its mounts, I attempted to stand.

"Kailas, hold us steady."

"But I thought you wanted me to evade…."

"Changed my mind."

He looked back at me with a confused expression, but upon seeing me slide a thermobaric warhead onto the tip of the launcher in my arms, quickly turned back to the directional monitors.

I shouldered open the vehicle's top hatch and emerged into the outside air. The screens inside the armored car had given a false sense of forward motion. We were puttering along at forty or fifty miles per hour. Whatever vehicle the rebels had up-armored to make this automotive monstrosity had clearly not been designed with such weight in mind.

The pilot overhead continued toying with us; he fired only short bursts of 30x165mm rounds from the autocannons on the helicopter's stubby wings, forcing Kailas to swerve each time they struck alongside us.

As I raised the RPG's optical sight to my eye, trying to frame the chopper in the reticle, my peripheral vision caught another movement overhead.

A second helicopter approached from the opposite side of the lake. In case the odds weren't tipped against us enough already. I pinched my eyes shut and cursed.

Kailas cut our vehicle tightly, the car bounding onto the gravel causeway leading to the fortress.

It was as though I could sense the pilots' sudden change in temperament. What had begun as such a simple objective as to warrant some lighthearted target practice had suddenly become a time-sensitive one: If we managed to get into the castle, they'd be forced to destroy another national landmark and expend untold amounts of ordnance just to destroy one homemade armored car.

Both helicopters began unloading their fearsome payload at us. A flurry of rockets and an ungodly spray of autocannon fire slapped dirt, flame and dust chasing us as we wound our way around the stronghold's knoll.

Kailas swung us towards the fortress's gatehouse. Doing some quick ocular calculations—gauging the width of our vehicle in relation to the distance between the rapidly approaching gatehouse pillars—I cursed and ducked, narrowly slipping back inside the vehicle before we slammed to an abrupt stop, the armored car jammed between the pylons.

Bits of shattered mud bricks flew forward as a cloud of dust blanketed our vehicle.

"No time to leave our insurance information," I said, dragging a dazed Kailas from the driver's seat and pushing him toward the hatch. "Move your ass, or so help me I'll whip you with this car's radio antenna."

Lugging the RPG, I followed Kailas out of the armored car. I hoped I didn't need to tell him to hide. I left him behind, sprinting through the remains of the building's vaulted hall. Bounding up a spiral stairway leading to the fortress's tallest minaret, I was accompanied by the helicopters' ballistic soundtrack— an auditory lovechild of the 1812 Overture and German death metal. Cold reality began to take hold, the icy bitch creeping up my spine, into the back of my skull, driving her barbed, venomous pincers into my thoughts. Every step I took brought me a second nearer to my inevitable death. There was no way out of it this time.

Nowhere left to run, no one willing to accept my surrender, no opportunity for smooth talk. Following the crumbling stairway before me as it twisted toward the sky, the sand underfoot like the salt-shaker dustings of a broken hourglass, I became incensed. Indignant at the thought of being killed here, after all the near-misses I'd survived over the years. On the verge of successfully escaping with our lives, only to be bested by some bloated Soviet helicopter. I was angry at Assad for not stepping down when the war first began. I was angry at the Sunni Islamists for poisoning the rebel cause. Hell, I was angry at Kailas for being so fucking helpless. But most of all, in that moment, inexplicably, I was enraged by that petulant woman who had written that nasty opinion piece ridiculing my Cairo article. I began to narrate aloud my response—one I knew now I would never get around to writing.

"Ma'am, I'd first like to apologize for your lamentable experience attempting to read my recent article on the Arab Spring uprisings in Cairo. We at the *Herald* simply expect those of your IQ to skip over challenging news articles such as this one on your way to the comics, with all those bright colors and simple words. It's a formidable leap to go from Doonesbury to hard journalism, and clearly, not everyone reacts to a challenge in an adult manner. It's likely the fault of one of your caretakers in the group home for leaving you alone with something as sharp and pointy as a pencil. You could have hurt yourself."

I double-checked the fit of the warhead in the launcher as I leapt up, step after step. Breathing had become a struggle, air coming hard and in shallow rasps. I continued anyway.

"Though I appreciate thoughtless feedback the way you welcome sausage-sized enemas, next time, keep your malicious, asinine drivel to yourself, you plebian window-licker."

God, Kailas was right. I had lost my touch. My razor wit had become dull. I shook off my doubt and tried to finish my response.

"To your accusation that I've never been to Egypt, I assure you, I've been there. I was in Cairo when I wrote that article. I've been shot at in Cairo. I've been stabbed in Cairo. I bled for that story, you illiterate troglodyte."

I stumbled, but caught myself with my left hand and righted myself quickly. A tracer round whined overhead, sinking into a nearby wall and leaving behind a smoldering hole the size of a fist. I swallowed a long breath as I bounded up the final stairs.

"With that in mind, please do the journalism community an enormous favor and switch from writing criticisms of that which you do not understand to something more fitting for your skill set—like fellating cacti."

It felt therapeutic to get all that off my chest. Perhaps it was immature and clumsily worded, but I didn't want to die without getting the last word in.

A rocket whistled by, striking the far side of the fortress and blowing out a wall. The helicopters continued their onslaught, punching holes in the mud brick with their cannons, sweeping in a steady arc towards one another, canvassing the entire place. Arriving at the top of the stairway, I found an aperture large enough to fire through, swung the RPG to my shoulder, and looked through the sight.

I flashed back to Afghanistan. I'd seen mujahideen fighters attempt to shoot down our helicopters with RPG-7s, and had even been aboard a Chinook that had narrowly evaded taking one squarely on the chin. I remembered it clearly; I'd pissed my last clean pair of pants on laundry day. I spent that afternoon waiting, in the buff, for the fabric to air dry. My legs got sunburned so badly I spent the next few days with the suffering, bent-legged saunter of a saddle-chafed cowboy.

That said, they'd still missed. Every RPG I'd seen launched at a target beyond a couple hundred yards had missed. These Hinds were well outside that range, and moving. And I had only one shot. Assuming I did manage to tag one, our only hope would be that the other pilot would then realize the cost-to-benefit ratio of killing us was too high, and would leave us alone.

That even sounded unlikely in my head.

A flying chunk of brick stung my leg as the helicopters' rounds struck closer. I didn't like the idea of killing those pilots. I didn't like the idea of being involved in this war or contributing to the killing. I'd been here ten months and hadn't fired one shot in anger.

But it was that, or die.

Both of us.

And I'd told Kailas I was going to get him home. He'd come to Syria to get me, and I would not be the reason he didn't make it out alive.

I fought my rising heartbeat and shaking arms as I lined up the shot, trying to remember any little kernel of wisdom related to firing the RPG.

The wind. Remember the wind.

The fins on the warhead cause it to turn *into* the wind—not with it. I adjusted my aim downwind as the helicopters neared one another. I squeezed the trigger.

Boom. Woosh. The warhead disappeared into the darkness.

That's when the wind quit blowing. Dead calm, as though Poseidon had taken a sharp breath and held it. The round went straight—right where I'd aimed it, but without any wind, it didn't cut back toward the helicopters as I'd hoped. It flew well outside the wing of the helicopter on my right.

It was a farcical denouement to our great escape. The sum of everything we'd been through amounted in that final moment to absolutely nothing. We would die here. Bodies shredded and left to rot in the sun and surf, just another pair of casualties buried somewhere inside a staggering statistic.

Suddenly, the helicopter I'd missed dipped hard—the pilot surprised by the warhead ripping past his cockpit. The craft's blades clipped the underside of his companion's helicopter, and the night sky erupted in orange flame—a calamitous bellow rolling toward us over the waves.

The fragmented remains of the two helicopters dropped into the surf, the pieces sinking out of sight amidst pools of flickering oil.

20
Tiny and Irregular Paychecks

Stepping down the stairway and dumping the RPG launcher in the sand, I said, "You hid under the car."

Kailas wiggled out from under the vehicle's steel plates like a well-dressed gopher. "So? Where else should I have hidden?"

"You hid under the one thing the pilots were aiming for. Tell me again, what do you do for a living? You oversee people, right? I mean, those people look to you for your leadership and wisdom?" I asked as I crawled atop the armored car, still firmly lodged between the brick pylons, and looked out over the reservoir. The cloud cover had dissipated, the first hint of early-morning sunlight warming the sandy plateau. The wash of the waves breaking against the citadel's dry moat blended with the cries of gulls overhead. A beauty rendered all the more beautiful by its proximity to our near-deaths. I took the deepest of breaths and let it out slowly, savoring its sweetness. "Gotta hand it to the ol' gal. She got us away from those Hinds as well as anyone could have hoped."

"It's a miserable piece of shit, Cogar. We could have taken any other vehicle from that garage and done better."

"Are you kidding? This baby is like a Dionysian bacchanalia, an absinthe-fueled orgy in the back room of a Parisian whorehouse, and a screaming electric-guitar solo played by Steve Vai as he parachutes from the rooftop of the Burj Al Arab hotel, all rolled into one. Now, you try outrunning one of those hinds in a Soviet Lada built out of old T-26 tank parts and melted pitchforks, maintained by a farmer named Igor who traded a goat and case of vodka for it. That's a challenge."

Kailas carefully untied a shoe, slipped it off, and dumped out a handful of fine sand. "Well I don't even care. I'm just glad that we're out of there and nobody's shooting at us anymore."

Taking a seat atop the car, I rubbed my leg where the sharp brick fragment had struck. My heart was still beating violently. "After all these years, I've got the knee cartilage of a 60-year-old Thai hooker."

"Spend a lot of time on your knees?" Kailas teased, dusting off his slacks.

"I'm a journalist. Goes without saying."

We spent the next hour chipping away the brick pylons anchoring our vehicle using a rusty tire iron and a sharp stone we found on the beach. When we'd managed to free it, we resumed our trek northward. Inside the car was silent; what was there to say? We'd both managed to survive impossible odds in the past 48 hours, and our exhaustion, in tandem with the likelihood of more obstacles in our future, had rendered both of us catatonic.

I glanced up at the two functional directional monitors and said, "You can pull over now."

"Why?" he shouted over the strained whine of our vehicle's engine as he leaned in, scrutinizing the flat land before us. "I'm all for keeping this bad boy flat out until we reach Europe."

"Mines," I said casually, tightening my belt a notch to gather the loose fabric of General Sabbagh's slacks.

"What?" he exclaimed, jamming his thumbs on the buttons, our vehicle stopping abruptly. The etiolated engine moaned as it wound down. "Landmines?"

I nodded as I flipped open the top hatch and looked out at the open, rock-strewn terrain. Fog rolled over the landscape, fringing the sides of the dirt road like floodwater. The morning sun hadn't risen above the tree line yet, and the road stood empty of vehicles, tire tracks, or footprints.

"A couple rules regarding landmines that you can devote to memory, Kailas," I yelled down the hatch. "First, don't be the first on the road in the morning—if anyone's going to bury fresh mines, they'll do it under cover of darkness." I paused, letting him consider what time of day it was. "Second, stick to pavement." Pause. "Third, don't listen to Cogar the next time he says to leave behind free flak jackets. They may be next to worthless on your person, but sitting on them while you're driving over what might turn out to be a minefield may just save your manhood."

Squirreling back inside the vehicle, I pushed open all the shooting ports and the hatch above. "Lastly, the shockwaves from mine blasts—like all things that make a really big boom—are amplified in cramped spaces like this one. Open a window, and you might only lose a couple limbs instead of your life."

"I hate everything about this, Cogar."

"Good. That's normal." I punched him in the arm playfully as I grabbed the case containing the polonium. "Come on. We've got some radioactive isotopes to bury."

"They'll just get more of it, you know," Kailas said, clambering out through the armored car's top hatch and following my footsteps as I marched toward a lone olive tree standing in a clearing.

"I know," I said, dropping to my knees and scratching at the dirt with my fingers. "But what else can we do? Assad wouldn't believe me even if I told him to his face that his right-hand man wanted him dead. We just bought the sonofabitch a little time, and the few remaining good guys on the front line a few more weeks to turn the tide." I pried at the corner of a rock.

"You really think this will help?" Kailas asked, reaching for a cluster of bright green olives hanging from the branches overhead.

I shook my head. "No. Even if Assad dropped dead tomorrow, I doubt anything would change enough to make a difference. His army is slowly being replaced by Iranian-trained militiamen from Pakistan, Iraq, and Afghanistan. The entire war is turning into a matter of proxies fighting proxies. Assad isn't even steering the ship anymore."

Wiping off an olive with his shirt sleeve, Kailas popped it into his mouth. His lips puckered, and he turned to spit out the bitter fruit. "I hate this place," he said. "Even nature hates this place." He dropped to his knees and began helping me dig the hole.

After a few minutes, I said, "He was an ophthalmologist."

"Who, Assad?"

I nodded. "He went to school to be an eye doctor. When his older brother wrapped his car around a tree, Assad got called home and placed in charge of the country. Amazing to think that a guy who has the blood of hundreds of thousands on his hands could have instead gone about his life prescribing eyewear."

"Sad, really," Kailas said, tugging on a root.

"Tragic. But it does make you wonder, doesn't it?" I asked, leaning back and propping my forearm on my knee. "If an educated man like Assad can transform from the head of the neighborhood watch into a sadistic dictator, what's stopping anyone from turning into a bloodthirsty animal? Is it an inherent part of humankind? A disease we all have that lays dormant until an opportunity arises?"

Kailas answered abruptly, "No. It's not. There's no instinctive human trait that makes us killers, goddammit. Educated or otherwise, Assad was a murderer from the minute he took his first breath. He may have kept it in check because society forced him to, but what he's doing today is motivated by his greed, his lust for power, and his own sadistic pleasure. Those aren't innate characteristics of people, they're aberrations. He's not a bad apple, he's a fucking walnut that got mixed in with the apples."

I picked up an exhumed earthworm and let it wriggle on my palm. "Well, if that's the case, there are an awful lot of walnuts that have gotten mixed into the bag. Some of the people I've seen out here...man, you wouldn't believe it even if you met them. You start out thinking everyone is just another Joe Normal from suburbia. But some of them, they lose it when the cameras turn off and the crowd's attention drifts elsewhere. In this line of work, you get assigned to places where order, rules, every semblance of logic disappear, and you're the only one expected to keep humanity's rulebook in your nightstand. Some people can't handle that. They may be educated, religious, or disciplined, but when they see the opportunity to drop the guise of civility, they want a taste. And that taste eventually turns into a ravenous, uncontrollable hunger."

I poked the earthworm until it stretched to its full length. "It starts slow. Maybe a guy witnesses a murder out in the field, only instead of being horrified, he feels a little tingle down below the belt. He knows he should feel ashamed. Society has taught him what is right and wrong, at least in general terms. But then he realizes that out here, he gets a free pass. No one's watching, and the ones who are have seen and done worse. The transformation begins. Maybe he pays a local girl for sex that night. A desperate cure for intolerable loneliness, that's all. But what happens when he discovers that she doesn't have a family, and the police, if there are any, don't care what happens to her?"

Kailas shook his head. "No. Cogar, stop this. I don't need to hear any more."

"Let me finish," I said, gently pinching the earthworm between my fingers and returning it to the soil. I watched as it urgently worked its way below the surface. "You wonder why I am the way I am? Why Cogar is always the pessimistic misanthrope bringing down the mood at Thanksgiving dinner? Hear me out. This guy, he's intrigued by the lack of consequences in this little war zone of ours. So he wraps his hands around this girl's neck, this nobody, this insignificant little soul born in the wrong country at the wrong time, and next thing, a white bread suburbanite with a minivan sitting in the airport parking garage is hauling a dead body down his hotel fire escape, soon to hastily bury the evidence of his crime in an unmarked grave. And no one will ever know. Rape, murder, pedophilia, necrophilia—every corner of the unplumbed possibilities of human depravity suddenly begin to solidify, crystallize in this vacuum."

I scooped up a pebble and threw it toward the armored car.

"Some of them even learn to justify it," I said. My voice had lost its fire, memories washing up like jetsam I'd thrown overboard years before. "I once had to share a room with this scrawny little NGO worker who would pay South Ossetian soldiers to escort him into Georgian villages they'd razed. He'd have them find decapitated bodies of villagers for him so he could beat off. He'd say it was just his life away from home. No harm in that, he'd say. His wife would never know. He'd get off the phone with her and his kids at night, and then he'd head out, straightaway, to do his illicit business. To him, every trip out of the country was just some sort of Vegas vacation where everything said and done stayed there, regardless of who got killed or fucked or abused."

I glanced at Kailas. His eyes were fastened to the dirt, his jaw locked, forehead drawn in deep creases.

"When you see this stuff happen, you begin to realize that the lines you've drawn between here and there, them and us, they don't exist," I said. "War is just a microcosm of humanity, one that works like a Petri dish to cultivate the bacteria, bringing the detritus hiding out among our species to the surface. I'm convinced that people—those obscene, irrational creatures—are the same no matter where you go."

I twisted my back until it popped, but an ache remained. "During WWII, Japan's Unit 731 vivisected human beings—men, women, children, thousands of them—without anesthesia. They did it under the guise of scientific advancement. That was less than a century ago. And you know what? The golden beacon of morality, the United fucking States, pardoned those who did it because we were more interested in their findings than in punishing them for their crimes. Both parties did it because they didn't think anyone would find out. This sort of thing isn't unique to one nation or one culture. History is riddled with examples of civilized people doing barbarous things. So what does that say about us—you and me, Kailas? Is peace a fallacy? Is morality malleable? Are we just fooling ourselves thinking that evil is something we can overcome?"

Kailas sniffed and adjusted his stare to the armored car in the distance. His sleeves were rolled to his elbows and his hands and knees were besmirched with fresh dirt. It was a good look for the old man.

He let out a defeated sigh. "I don't have the answer to that, Cogar."

I suddenly felt apologetic about my pessimistic rant. "I don't know that anyone does," I said, slapping his back. I didn't want Kailas to mistakenly take my polemic as an attack against him or the life he'd lived. I just wanted him to see the world as I saw it, to take a step off the primrose path and see the world with a critical eye.

With the hole deep enough to fit the polonium's case, I shoved it inside and asked, "So I got evicted, huh?"

Kailas piled on the loose dirt. "Kinda weird that that was the first thing that came to mind when I thought we were going to die. I guess it was as though I'd been holding on to it like a grocery list or a household chore I intended to get to, and felt I needed to clear it from my mind before I died."

"You've got a strange sense of priority, old friend."

He continued. "I couldn't fit your mattress in the station wagon, but I managed to get most of your other stuff back to the house. I stuffed it in Page's old room. It almost filled up the back seat of the car. How you go through life owning so little?"

"Your tiny and irregular paychecks have been a big help in maintaining my minimalist lifestyle, Kailas," I replied, hiding my surprise that I'd actually been evicted. Hasan, that perfidious bastard. You live in the same apartment for almost twenty years, you expect some preferential treatment. Or at least a little flexibility on the rent due date. It'd only been ten months, after all.

I stood and tamped the dirt down with my socked foot. Reaching into my pocket, I withdrew the hood ornament from General Sabbagh's Bentley and screwed it into the freshly overturned earth. "Looks like we're going home together after all. All the way home. To your home, specifically. You don't think Dannielle would mind if I stayed with you guys for a week or two, would she?"

******

Helmand Province, Afghanistan
December, 2009

I made fun of vegetarians before I went to Afghanistan. But my time there taught me an appreciation for plant matter and karma. Tawfik didn't understand what my problem was with the shoe-leather meat; you just had to pick around the maggots. Whenever I would grouse about a meal or complain about my self-induced diet of green tea and bread, the elderly Pashtun man would turn to me, raise an eyebrow, and say, "Okay, tonight, you make the supper."

Tawfik worked as a local guide for the humanitarian demining operations in the area and had been gracious enough to invite me to stay with him while I worked on my article covering the impact of landmines on the country's socioeconomic health. His black beard was stippled with strands of gray, the wrinkles in his sun-weathered face so deep they made it look like he was wearing one of those caricatured Ronald Reagan Halloween masks. But he had kind eyes, and laughed often, and despite speaking little English, made the time I spent with him go by quickly. I spent several days placing my feet in the exact imprints left by his sandals as he expertly navigated the tawny grass and gravel of the minefields.

During their ten-year occupation of the country in the 1980s, the Soviets, frustrated with their military might being thwarted by resilient mujahideen hiding out in the country's massive network of cave systems, had waged a brutal depopulation campaign of which landmines were a major component. The U.S. State Department estimated between ten and thirty million of the nasty little bastards had been sown in Afghanistan. That ranged from anti-tank mines to toe-poppers—the latter, as the name would suggest, equipped with just enough explosive to blow off a hand or foot, perfect for creating disabled, disfigured civilians that would only drain the country's fragile economy. Tawfik pointed out a cluster of such mines on the bank of a gravel-lined wadi during one of our walks.

"Butterflies," he said.

They were small—maybe a little larger than an adult's hand— a washed-out green color, and looked as though they had wings. The name fit. Tawfik swept his arms toward the sky and fluttered his hands as if to illustrate falling confetti, his loose-fitting shalwar kameez billowing as the wind picked up.

"They dropped them from aircraft?" I asked. He nodded, though I knew he hadn't understood much if any of what I had just said.

"They look like toys," I said. That was part of the plan, too. The Soviets knew that kids would be drawn to these mines. Nothing worked harder to dishearten an enemy than striking at its children, and it destroyed the next generation of would-be fighters.

For a few minutes, we stared at that cluster of innocuous-looking mines, discolored from years spent in the sun but still deadly. I glanced at my guide. He made no sound, but tears dripped from his cheeks, following the path of the wrinkles in his skin like the first drops of desert rain. I was bewildered. The old adage 'men don't cry' was never more true than with Pashtun men. As hard as the mountain passes they inhabited, they judged a man on three things: his skill with a rifle, the length and thickness of his facial hair, and his ability to withstand pain. Tears were taboo; they revealed a man's weakness.

"Tawfik, you okay?"

"Walid," he whispered.

"I don't understand," I said, trying to determine what evocative memory could have triggered this perpetually cheerful man's tears.

He gestured as though rocking a baby in his arms, and then tapped his chest.

"Your son? Daughter?"

"Son. Walid," he affirmed. "Not toy," he said, pointing at the pile of mines.

I set my jaw and looked at my feet. I understood, now. He'd lost his son to the mines, and he'd since made it his mission to keep others from experiencing his loss. Looking out at the miles of rocky ground flanked by imposing snowcapped mountains, all of it riddled with explosives, I knew, as I'm sure he knew, how fruitless it all was. It would take several lifetimes to make even a subtle difference, but he was trying.

When I was younger, I would probably have regarded a man like Tawfik as a simpleton, an uneducated third-world peasant with only a few teeth and an acrid, rotting-onion smell about him.

But having spent time with him in these fields and in his home, saw his humility, his patience, and how he had buried this immense injustice and profound pain beneath his inexplicable optimism, I recognized now that such men were among the most stalwart and admirable of any I'd met. How could anyone withstand living in this inhospitable environment after losing their family to invading armies, sickness, malnourishment, and landmines, yet freely smile and offer what little they had to a complete stranger?

Tawfik stamped a foot, let out a long breath, and resumed walking.

That night, we lay on opposite sides of his small mud-brick hut—Tawfik with an arm draped over his eyes, me compiling the previous days' notes by the flickering light from an oil lamp. We said nothing. Only the sound of my pen scribbling on paper, the popping of the flame in the fireplace, and the crackle of falling hail filled the small room.

The steady crumble of the ice storm was suddenly interrupted by roaring explosions in the distance. I rushed to extinguish my light, thinking Taliban forces might have been attacking. Tawfik laughed.

"What's so funny?" I asked, stepping to the door and looking outside, pulling my leather jacket tighter to my core as the cold came in. My breath condensed in a white cloud that obscured my vision, but I could still make out the dusting of cherry-size ice chunks bouncing atop the sandy earth.

"Minesweeper," Tawfik said. He lifted a foot into the air and wiggled his toes.

"I know, I've been here with you for a week. I kinda figured that's what you've been doing," I said.

He shook his head, his smile wide. Illustrating the falling hail with his hands, he made a gesture like an explosion. The falling hail was triggering the mines.

"Allah's minesweeper," he said. "Tomorrow is good day."

The next morning, seated before a grid of fluorescent mason's line stretched between wood stakes outlining the demining lanes, halfway through an interview with an English minesweeper, I heard a pop come from just beyond a nearby hill. Nothing huge, just a little more than a gunshot or an exploding firework. But my interview subject stood to look, the other men in the lanes depositing their gear in the sand as they went to investigate. Seconds later, they returned carrying a man by the wrists and knees. Swinging as they walked was one singed leg and one mangled stump where the man's foot had been.

"Get him in the truck," the foreman cried.

I approached the wounded man and felt my gut shrivel, like taking a line drive to the genitals. "Tawfik. Oh Christ, man."

He waved a hand at me dismissively, as though the grisly wound was only a scratch. Seeing that my expression wasn't changing, the old man smiled at me through his apparent pain.

"Okay. Tonight, you make the supper."

I climbed inside the cab of the truck, my mind hazy as I watched the men load Tawfik into the bed. Someone slammed the tailgate and slapped the rear side panel, letting us know they were ready. The driver, face red as he dropped the shifter into drive, said something to me, his tone resentful. I didn't hear him. Under my breath, I recited:

If they just went straight they might go far;
They are strong and brave and true;
But they're always tired of the things that are,
And they want the strange and new.

21
In the Jungle With Little Boys

Manbij, Syria
30 kilometers south of Turkish border
June 2013

Coal-black smoke filled the armored car's interior, the overburdened engine overheating—oil starved. We'd put the fortified jalopy through its paces, and it simply had nothing more to give.

"You suppose there's a place around here we could grab something to eat, Cogar? I'm starving," Kailas said before launching into a coughing fit, waving a hand in front of his face to clear away the exhaust.

"It's been less than six hours since we ate last, Kailas, and you've been complaining about your hunger for at least three of them. You're like one of those laboratory chimps that keeps pressing the reward button in his cage until he dies of morbid obesity."

He swallowed hard, his eyes watering. "I eat my feelings, and lately, I've had some really intense feelings. Terror, rage, panic...that sort of thing. Besides, this smoke is unbearable."

"All right. Pull over. We should be out of the most kinetic areas by now, anyway. Let's find you a hot dog stand."

Kailas angled the car under a tattered awning, steel scraping against the building's concrete side. The impact canted one of our navigation cameras.

"How does such a terrible driver manage to keep the same crappy station wagon for 20 years? That thing's gotta look like a crushed pop can by now," I said, flinging open the hatch. Finding the awning blocking our way out, I set to work tearing the fabric to create an exit.

"My car has these things called 'windows' that really help with the whole driving concept," he shot back. "And Chicago has streets without mortar holes in them. That helps too."

We disembarked, and Kailas began trying to communicate his hunger to a pair of teenage boys sitting nearby, gesturing at his mouth as though holding an imaginary fork and shrugging his shoulders. They looked at me for an explanation. I shrugged apologetically.

Kailas groaned, "God, even another lukewarm vegetarian MRE would taste like foie gras about now."

The percussive thump of a kick drum, followed by a hard-driving riff from an electric guitar, boomed from a vehicle's stereo, growing in volume as it approached. AC/DC's "You Shook Me All Night Long" thundered from the cab of an up-armored pickup truck—the calling card of Western military contractors pulling a personal security detail—as a small convoy rolled into the village, pulling to a stop in a broad semicircle. Surrounded by an entourage of photographers, translators, and musclebound bodyguards in Oakley sunglasses and black polo shirts, a familiar face emerged.

"No way," I said, groaning and burying my face in my arms, leaning against our car.

"Someone you know?" Kailas asked over his shoulder.

I didn't raise my head, my words muffled as I said, "For the sake of efficiency, let's just say that we should handle any communications with her as if she were an ex-lover of mine."

Kailas sighed. "So she's an ex-lover of yours."

"I didn't say that. I just said we should treat her like she is."

"Then I'll do what I always do when you run into one of your old flames. I'm going to go hide around the corner until danger passes," Kailas said. True to his word, he promptly disappeared behind the nearest building.

Though I'd known I would inevitably run into Sally Parker at some point in my travels, I'd not expected a reunion so soon following our awkward valedictory in Cairo.

Before Egypt, I'd only viewed Sally as the stereotypical wannabe warrior reporter—one who'd built her reputation on interviews of Powerpoint rangers at forward operating bases and glamor shots of herself standing before shot-up military equipment in her clean, blue Kevlar helmet and vest. In Cairo, I'd learned there was another layer buried beneath the facade. Sally also possessed an insatiable, almost violent sex drive, and a misunderstanding of the word no.

"You keep working on finding us some grub," I said to Kailas before realizing he was already out of earshot. So I whispered to myself, "I'm going to go sell my soul for a ride to the border."

I took a deep breath and approached the crowd directly. Two of Sally's security guards stepped in front of her, their rifles at the low ready, but upon recognizing me, she tapped them on the shoulders and shook her head. Removing her helmet, she walked toward me as I dragged a pair of kitchen chairs from the rubble of a bombed-out building toward an upended wooden cable spool in the street. Setting a chair on both sides of the spool, I sat down.

Sally approached and stood before me, her brown hair pulled into a ponytail, flak jacket covering her chest. She was a short thing, full-bodied and with features that would have guaranteed she wouldn't have been the last woman to get picked up at a bar, but also such that she wouldn't likely be the first, either. Her acerbic personality made the second likelihood a certainty.

"Pretty hot out for so much armor. Must be uncomfortable to be so safe," I said, trying to make it sound like just a little lighthearted teasing between old friends. My voice, flat and unenthusiastic, betrayed me.

"Want me to take it off?" she asked seductively, pulling the hook-and-loop straps from her shoulders and letting the vest drop to the dirt. Beneath, the top three buttons of her shirt were unbuttoned, sweat beading on her skin where her shirt parted. I tried my best not to stare at her cleavage as she leaned forward and sat down across from me, letting her hair down.

If she had changed since our last meeting, I could only tell by the fact that she hadn't tackled me to the dirt and straddled me yet.

Struggling with the words, I said, "Sally, I need a favor from you."

"You? Asking me for a favor? You must be desperate."

"You have no idea. Look, my editor and I just need a ride back to the Turkish border."

She ignored me, her eyes shamelessly exploring every inch of my body as she seductively chewed her bottom lip. "I'd been hearing rumors that you'd gone native. But the suit, the good looks walking the line between slovenly and rugged...looks like the same old Cogar to me."

"Same old Cogar," I said, arms outstretched as I tipped back in my chair.

After a moment of pretend-contemplation, she whispered, "What's this trip across the border worth to you?"

"I don't have any money, if that's what you're getting at." I knew what would come next, and began looking for a clean place to stow my clothes that would keep them from getting stolen while I paid for our trip with my body.

She smiled diabolically. "I'll let you ride back with us, but only if you agree to an interview," she said, sliding an MP3 voice recorder from her pocket and turning it on.

"You're serious?" I'd expected her to ask for a quick romp in the back seat of her fixer's car, not an interview. Oddly, I'd have been more comfortable with the former.

"Yes. And an apology for Cairo."

"I've got nothing to apologize for. If I recall, you said some nasty, mean-spirited things to me. Something along the lines of 'Cogar, you're an arrogant, impotent, gutless man-slut.'"

"I only said those things after you left me hanging on a coat hook—for six hours."

I swallowed a laugh. "God, it took you six hours to get down from there? That's...well that's sad. But, in my defense, I was only protecting myself from sexual assault," I said, leaning toward the recorder and enunciating every word, watching her cheeks flush. She fumbled with the device, pausing it.

"You led me to believe you shared my feelings," she whispered.

"I'm sorry for the confusion."

"So you mean to tell me you felt nothing for me at all?" She slid her hand across the table and touched my fingertips softly, raising an eyebrow.

I looked at her hand, sighed, and shifted mine off the table.

"Sally, is this really what you wanted to talk to me about? Or can we get down to the interview? Sorry to be brusque, but I've been shot at an awful lot over the past few months, which has just played hell on the quality of my sleep."

"You sure that's the reason you haven't slept well? Or is it because there's an absence of suitable harlots in this war zone to warm your bed?" she asked, her fingernails digging into the wood spool.

I rubbed my eyes. "Nope, haven't had any trouble finding myself in the company of harlots."

She looked away, trying hard to sequester a fit of rage as she restarted her voice recorder and planted her hands in her lap. She forced a thin smile.

"Let's start over, okay? What was your reason for going to Syria?" she asked.

"The nightlife and the beaches."

"I'm serious, Cogar." She tapped a rapid rhythm on the spool with her pointer and middle fingers, like a postal clerk in some 19th century frontier town tapping out an urgent message on a telegraph register.

"So am I."

Sally balled her hand into a fist and tapped her forehead with it, emphasizing each word as she said, "Syria is almost entirely landlocked."

"I was misinformed."

She stared at me, her expression indignant, until I relented.

"Okay, you know what inspired me to come here? A kid."

"A kid? Anyone in particular?"

"Just some kid. A green-eyed refugee boy on the news. But, I don't know, there was something about him that stuck." My eyes drifted across the rooftops of the village. "Now, I expect every time I turn around to see him. That very kid. Wearing that same expression. Dammit if I don't still see the look on that kid's face when I close my eyes."

Sally seemed discomfited by my sudden honesty, turning back to her legal pad for her next question. The pen in her hand looked new, I noticed, and the pad was without coffee stains or dirt.

"Do you find that being a freelancer—and I'm assuming as a result having fewer resources at your disposal—has negatively impacted the quality of your reporting?"

"Has carrying the *Los Angeles Times'* credit card made your reporting any better?" I countered, glancing at her sizeable entourage. Behind me, I could hear Kailas exchange shouts with the teenagers who he had suddenly decided weren't being forthcoming about the whereabouts of the nearest food supply.

She tossed her hair and looked at me, ignoring my pointed response. "Some in the journalism community have called you a modern day Indiana Jones for your cavalier exploits and distinctive, immersive style."

"That's ridiculous," I replied. "I'm not a professor, I'm not here to steal artifacts, and I don't get my jollies from hanging out in the jungle with little boys."

She smirked, but continued. "You disappeared for months, and rumor has it you joined the rebels on the front lines as a soldier. Did this in any way affect your objectivity when reporting on the war?"

I snorted. "Objectivity is one of those fabled golden rules taught in collegiate J-schools, no different than the illusion of blind justice in law or philanthropy in business. Do I try to avoid injecting personal bias into my writing? Of course. I'd be a pretty shitty journalist if I didn't. But no one is as objective as they think."

"Okay, but *why* did you do it?" she asked. "You've been in this business for years. So what was it about this war in particular that caused you to pick up a rifle?"

That one made me pause. Like lurching and stumbling through a monochromatic, demon-riddled nightmare, my time in Syria, even with its horrifying revelations, had left me mostly numb. Accepting. Dismayed, yet somehow unsurprised. But like waking from such a dream to find oneself in clean sheets, the sun shining rapturously through the window, pulled back to the surface from the depths of one's despair, I could now look back on where I'd been. It was all so much more grotesque in the sunlight.

When I didn't come back with a snarky response, Sally looked up at me attentively.

Finally, I spoke softly, "I think I'd lost my sense of purpose." I scooted my chair back and rubbed my chin, surprised when I found it clean-shaven. "It's easy to get caught up in first-world problems. Our homes, our jobs, our relationships..." I glanced at Sally. "People forget that the rest of the world, down below, the dark regions they don't even like to see on the news, scrapes on, clinging to survival, even as they scurry about, convincing themselves that all their trivial, privileged bullshit really, really matters. I think I'd just become frustrated trying to convince those people to look around them, to see that the struggles of those in faraway places actually mattered. I've spent my whole career trying to do that, and I don't know that it's ever worked. So, I did the only thing I could think to do: I dropped my pen and picked up a med kit. The last few months have given me perspective, if nothing else. And I've become intimate with the strife of the people here unlike anyone else could by simply coming and going."

Sally set her pen on the makeshift table and looked at me.

"That's beautiful, Grant."

Resting my knuckles against the wooden spool, I applied pressure until each one cracked in turn. "No, it's not. It's really fucking ugly, actually. It's the ugliest thing in the whole fucking world, standing knee-deep in desolation, looking back at my countrymen, oblivious on their golden hilltop. Fuck it, though. Maybe a Hollywood starlet will appear on one of those commercials asking the middle class to donate ten cents a day to the Syrian children, or maybe someone will get the brilliant idea to start selling trite rubber bracelets with some politically charged acronym on it. SS for 'save Syria', maybe. Oh, that'd be perfect, wouldn't it? Nothing says 'I care about the children' like dollar-store jewelry with history's most evil paramilitary organization's title on it."

Sally clicked her pen and placed it atop her notepad, then turned off her recorder.

"Thank you for taking the time to speak with me, Cogar." She extended her hand, and I shook it firmly. "I'll see you around, I'm sure," she said, buttoning her shirt, slipping her protective vest over her head, and turning to walk back to her car, pocketing her voice recorder.

"Well, we're riding back to the border together, right?" I called after her.

She stopped and turned, wearing a sinister grin, and said, "Hurts to be deceived, doesn't it?"

She jumped into the cab of a truck alongside one of her guards, reached a hand out the window, and waved goodbye as they drove away.

22
All Risk, No Reward

Outside the crumbling remains of an orphanage, Kailas and I sat cradling tin mugs of instant coffee and watched children in the distance gathering copper and steel from detonated rockets. Deep ruts in the once-fallow fields left by heavy military vehicles still wound chaotically across the earth, like the stitching on a baseball that had been run over by a lawnmower. They stood out from the stubborn tufts of green like contaminated cuts that never heal, only fester.

I looked at my mug doubtfully after a sip and ran my tongue over my teeth in hopes of wiping away the lingering taste.

"What? Not good enough for you? This is still better than the stuff in the *Herald*'s break room," Kailas said.

"Pretty sure we've got the cure for cancer growing in those coffee pots."

Licking my lips thoughtfully, I said, "I like my coffee the way I like my women. Fresh. And smooth. And hot. And preferably, cheap."

Letting his cup's steam warm his face, Kailas said, "I thought you'd given up this stuff, anyway."

"Eh, pure living wasn't for me. And I left the last of my ya-dom in my other pants. We could always go back and get them. I'm sure that whole thing with Sameera and the polonium was just one big misunderstanding."

Kailas chuckled. "Yeah, I'm sure she'd forgive you for tossing her in the cesspool, too. Every relationship has its little hiccups, after all."

"I should have left a note for her husband, apologizing for his poor luck. It takes a special kind of stupid to marry that grade of crazy."

A rooster cackled somewhere nearby, the laughs of the children filling the evening air.

"You know what?" Kailas said, scooping a flake of soot out of his cup with his pinky finger. "I'm not unhappy right now. I feel guilty saying this, but I feel, I don't know, alive."

"Yeah, that's the appeal."

"That's what keeps you doing this?"

I set my mug down on a slab of concrete between my feet and looked at my mentor. The dying sunlight made him look younger—the shadows hiding the dark patches below his eyes and the ladder of wrinkles on his forehead.

"Let me tell you a little bedtime story, Kailas. Before Saddam Hussein was captured, an Iraqi scientist defected to the States, claiming that Hussein had a biological weapons program underway. After you sent me to Iraq in 2006, I tracked that guy down. He admitted to me that there was no such program, and that he'd lied to help bring down Hussein. Colin Powell had testified before the UN that this program was real, and now here I was, unraveling the entire story, sitting with this bearded guy drinking chai tea like we're discussing the weather."

The top of the sun finally glided behind the horizon. The moon and stars became the only light as the buildings nearby blacked out.

I continued, "I revealed the story I had to the major networks, and CNN jumped on it with both feet. They signed the standard exclusivity contracts, and swore to only use the photos I provided on their website and news program—giving me full credit. Turned out to be a load of horseshit, and my photos, with CNN's logo stamped on them, ran in damn near every newspaper and magazine from New York to LA before I even got the story to you."

Dumping the last of his coffee, now lukewarm, into the dirt, Kailas said, "You could have sued."

"Sure, there were grounds for a lawsuit, but I didn't have money to pay my rent—as you've seen—let alone hire a lawyer to go after a giant media company. So I barely covered my costs, but made a media conglomerate thousands." I shrugged. "It's part of being a freelancer. We come to places like this, assume all the risk, and earn none of the reward." I felt a smile forming and let it come. "But one thing they can't take away is that feeling you're experiencing right now—that unshakeable gratitude just to be breathing, that immense thankfulness to have a hot cup of coffee in your hand, kids playing nearby, and a moment of peace where no one is shooting at you. That's why I keep doing this. Because there's nothing else quite like it."

****

Moundou, Chad
January 2006

Jonathan didn't like my face. That was the first thing the British expat told me upon our introduction outside Moundou Airport. I apparently reminded the craggy Royal Marine veteran of a neighbor he'd once had back in Rutland—an insufferable lout who regularly mowed over Jonathan's blueberry bush seedlings and drove a yellow sportscar with no muffler.

My fixer hurled my leather duffel bag into the bed of his Mahindra pickup truck—the rusty steel long ago replaced with sun-warped 2x6s bolted to the vehicle's frame. I spent the first leg of our journey listening to him complain about the shrapnel wound in his leg while he chain-smoked State Express 555s—the only English cigarettes he could regularly purchase in-country.

"I found you a decent hotel," he said after a long silence, flicking the tip of his cigarette and sending the glowing ash through the open window. "I know the owner. He's an obnoxious little prick, and I wouldn't eat any food he's prepared—blighter picks his nose incessantly—but he's got the best-stocked bar in the city and the sheets are clean."

"That's great," I whimpered, gripping the cab's oh-shit handle as a bicyclist tried to cross the street, cutting in front of us and missing our vehicle's front fender by inches. Jonathan locked up the brakes and pinned his palm against the horn.

"Gordon Bennet, bloody pillocks trying to end their miserable lives by laying themselves out on the hood of my vehicle. I've half a mind to oblige the grotty bastards."

And so it went, with the surly Brit displaying an imaginative collection of curses and oaths as we rumbled along, dodging careless drivers and pedestrians, just surviving in a country where the rules of the road had long ago devolved into anarchy.

"Must you do that?" Jonathan asked, eyes darting from sidewalk to sidewalk as if anticipating an attack.

"Do what?" I was confused. What could I possibly have done to irritate him? I'd only met the man five minutes before.

"Crack your knuckles like bleeding popping corn. Twiddle your thumbs if you feel the need, but do it quietly. You're upsetting my calm."

His calm? I'd never met a man who embodied tranquility less than my fixer.

"Oh, sorry."

The paved roads soon lost their painted lines, shrinking in width until they dissolved into hard-packed, paprika-colored clay. When *we arrived at the hotel, Jonathan left me to fetch my own luggage, moving in a straight line for the building's downstairs bar.*

I took in my surroundings as my surroundings took me in. Pedestrians, dressed in baggy, brightly colored printed fabric, stopped in the streets to watch me, their expressions curious but distrustful. Below the women's headwraps and the men's buzzcut hair, chocolate-toned skin glistened with beaded sweat. I shuffled toward the hotel foyer, scanning the turquoise, balcony-enshrouded building. I coughed out a black fly.

I sidled up to my fixer at the bar and nodded at the bartender, the jaundice-eyed man drying a beer glass with a rag. I glanced around. The hotel's furniture revealed the country's colonial past, the French influence obvious in the drooping rush-seat chairs, the shoe-worn cabriole table legs, and the patinated corbels supporting the bar. The place was anchored at some point in the distant past; there'd been no call to modernize.

"He's buying," was all Jonathan could get out as he slammed back his first beer. Here, it was impossible to tell if a man was an alcoholic or merely battling the muggy heat. You could usually trust the bottled beer. The water? Not so much.

Eager to establish a schedule before my fixer became too inebriated to count on, I said, "Jonathan, you'd mentioned that you could put me in touch with Mahamat Nour. When do you think that meeting could take place?"

The looks of the few patrons at the bar followed by the harsh grip of my fixer's hand on my wrist instantly conveyed my mistake. A war was on, and loud talk of meeting with the Chadian rebel commander had crossed the threshold from controversial to dangerous.

"You mind speaking a little louder, you dolt? Christ." Jonathan took another swig of his beer. "It's going to take a little time to coordinate with his people, okay? You sit tight here, and with any luck, you'll be asking him stilted questions over a cup of coffee in the morning, all right?"

I nodded, embarrassed. I took my beer up to my room, sipping it as I watched the people in the street from my balcony. An hour later, Jonathan sauntered back to his truck. No one paid him a glance. Without the British accent, he was just another lanky black man in khakis. I wondered why he'd come here, why he would stay. It hardly seemed the sort of place that would be top of mind when looking for somewhere to retire.

My stomach grumbled. My head buzzed from the beer. I was too embarrassed to go back into the hotel lobby to ask where to go for food, replaying in my head how I'd announced to the world my plans for a clandestine meeting. I'd make a terrible secret agent. Still, I needed to eat. So I slung my bag over a shoulder and exited via a rickety stairway bolted to the backside of the building. The sun had begun to set, the African heat giving way to a pleasant cool, the dusty earth painted in magnificent aurulent and lavender strokes. I stopped to buy a banana and a mystery-meat kebab a few blocks away. That's when the overpressure from the explosion flattened the fabric of my shirt against my skin.

The hotel erupted in a cloud of flame, windows bursting outwards, glass shards slung into the dirt. I ran, first a few yards away from the explosion, and then back in the direction of the hotel. Black smoke drifted low. There were no screams, just a stunned silence. A cicada-like ringing hovered in my ears.

I tore at the rubble, pulling bodies free. Living? Dead? I couldn't tell. I turned around and Jonathan was there, administering first aid to those still fighting for breath. He looked at me and cursed. Furious. At first, I thought, enraged by this heinous act of wanton violence. But then I saw it. That sharp glimmer was directed at me. Resentful. Enraged. A white American, a stranger in a strange culture, had invited this attack. This bomb had been meant for me. And it had killed all these people, Jonathan's friends, parts of his life. All of them sacrificed for a stranger—a man with a face he didn't like.

Onlookers hovered nearby, jaws slack, hands held at their sides, paralyzed by the wreckage, the moaning of the wounded, the bodies laying like broken toys in the dirt.

"Don't just stand there, you gormless wazzocks, get me some bandages!"

I moved forward to help as he hefted an unconscious woman, missing both her legs below the knees, into the bed of his truck.

"Back off," he snarled. "This country doesn't need any more help from you."

As I watched him desperately scrambling to triage the wounded, familiar words played through my head.

> *They say: "Could I find my proper groove,*
> *What a deep mark I would make!"*
> *So they chop and change, and each fresh move*
> *Is only a fresh mistake.*

****

Manbij, Syria
June 2013

I awoke to the steady thump of artillery shells striking in the distance, my shirt plastered to my chest with cold sweat, my breathing rapid and shallow. Sitting up on my cot, I leaned against the concrete of the orphanage kitchen wall. For the first time in years, I felt I might weep. Just collapse into an inconsolable, childish bawling.

Syria was on its way to becoming a hellish wasteland with nothing redemptive left to salvage from its pitiful, rotten mire. My leaving felt as though I was betraying all that I'd fought for in the past ten months, and that I was abandoning the country to its ugly fate. Returning to the safety of Chicago, where I could walk across the street and buy a sandwich, run the faucet for a pure glass of water, and sleep under clean sheets each night felt unfair and hypocritical. It would be hard to stay here alone, without Kailas or Shukri, but I didn't know if I'd be able to return to the U.S. and look myself in the mirror.

Being inside an orphanage wasn't helping, either. I'd spent my fair share of lonely nights inside places like this as a kid, and the empathy I felt for the children here bordered on the intolerable. I'd had a rough go of it in my early years, but there hadn't been mortars raining down on me, and I always got my three square meals each day. These kids…God, these poor kids.

Footsteps, soft and careful, padded along the concrete floor. The only light came from a dim bare bulb several rooms over, illuminating the outline of a young girl as she approached. I suddenly noticed my ragged breathing and cleared my throat in an attempt to regain my composure. The girl plodded forward haltingly, clutching a dirty pink blanket to her chest as a corner dragged along the floor behind her.

She reached a hand out, but not to me. Her fingers danced in the darkness, and slowly, she turned toward the sound of my breathing. I looked into her eyes. They were empty, discolored, her corneas a hazy white.

She was blind.

I choked on fresh tears, the breath torn from my chest as though someone had centered a ball peen hammer on my sternum. She smiled, coming closer, moving her hand to my cheek. I leaned forward, and she wrapped her arms around my neck, patting my back reassuringly.

The tears came. I held on to that little girl as though she were my last handhold, as if I were a man clinging to the edge of a cliff, muscles burning, fingers slipping. And at that moment, I was.

But amidst this relentless suffering, the constant crippling fear, the perpetual agony of loss and death, this child was smiling and reassuring me. Everything was so horrible, but there was this girl. This smiling, innocent little person unwilling to bend under the crushing weight of the world, unable to feel self-pity for her miserable lot in life. I wasn't holding her; she was holding me. And in that moment, face buried in her shoulder, I felt all my self-loathing, my doubt, my cynicism, fall away. There was hope in this world, and even if I couldn't be the one to fix it all, this girl, and more like her, would.

23
A Tale of Two Asses

We set out the next morning at dawn, firing up the armored car and carefully navigating our way out of the city proper. The houses went from concrete block to something more akin to field stones—all of different sizes, rough, held together tenuously by crumbling mortar and a web of moss. It had a tranquil, bucolic feel about it—a reminder that no matter how turbulent the world might become, there would always be a quiet green pasture or orchard ignoring it all.

"You seem perky today," Kailas said. "You must have just needed a cup of coffee."

"Something like that."

"But really, you have a spring in your step, like the old Cogar has finally come back."

I turned to him and smiled sincerely. "I think I'm finally ready to go home."

"Best news I've heard since I set foot in this fucking country," Kailas said, beaming. His smile was quickly replaced by a scowl as the armored car's engine coughed and sputtered—out of gas and leaking oil like an English sports car. The vehicle rolled to a final stop outside a small farmhouse at the base of a tall hill.

"And from here, we push," I joked, sliding out the vehicle's top hatch and dropping into ankle-deep mud. My socked feet made squelching pops as I navigated to firmer ground.

"We're not leaving the car here, are we?" Kailas asked, following me out, but stopping his slide halfway down the side of the car when he realized the depth of the mud around us. "I mean, why don't we just track down some fuel and make a beeline to the border?" He grunted as he dangled against the car, too weak to pull himself back up, but still unwilling to accept defeat and drop into the morass below.

"Because every helicopter and tank crew in this country are on the lookout for a vehicle like this. It may not feel as safe, and it may take a little longer, but making ourselves out to be poor civilians riding farm animals should elicit little more than a giggle from anyone who would otherwise waste a perfectly good artillery round on us."

An elderly man wearing a keffiyeh and a threadbare wool suit jacket sauntered toward us. The property owner. As he neared, I gestured toward a small herd of feeble-looking donkeys inside a pen nearby, and then pointed at our armored car.

"Even trade?"

The farmer shook his head. Reaching a wrinkled hand toward my suit jacket, he touched the material before examining the lining. Behind me, I heard two size-ten loafers slap the mud, followed by a groan.

I emptied the pockets of my few remaining possessions and took the jacket off, handing it to the elderly farmer.

"How about now?"

He shook his head again, gesturing this time at my pants.

"Cogar, he wants the full suit. Take off your pants and let's get moving," Kailas said, carefully tiptoeing his way to drier ground.

"Easy for you to say," I countered. You're not the one who would have to ride a donkey through a fucking war zone in your underwear. I've witnessed public shamings more decent than that."

Reaching a lonely island of green grass, Kailas began stomping to free the mud from his shoes. "Just give it to him. We'll find you new clothes when we get to the border."

I stared angrily at the farmer as I slipped off my shirt and, unfastening my belt, dropped my pants; slipping them from my legs and folding them in half, I handed them over.

"It'd better not rain before then."

The farmer nodded, raising a single finger. One suit, one donkey.

Surprised, I turned and grinned devilishly at Kailas.

"Looks like you're going to have to hand over your clothes, too, old friend. That is, unless you're looking to ride double with a naked guy. Don't know what the Turkish border guards will think of that. It is Thursday, after all."

"What does that have to do with anything?" Kailas asked, pulling his arms to his chest as though protecting his shirt.

"Back in Kandahar, the troops had a running joke about Man Love Thursdays. The Islamic holy day of prayer falls on a Friday, so male fundamentalists would allegedly have sex with one another on Thursday to keep them from being distracted by lustful thoughts during prayer. Today's Thursday, and I don't want anyone getting the wrong idea about us, Kailas. Give the man your clothes and get your own fucking donkey."

With an exasperated sigh, Kailas looked to the farmer pleadingly. The farmer gestured toward Kailas's shirt and suppressed a grin.

Unbuckling his belt and reluctantly slipping off his shoes and pants, Kailas said, "This is ridiculous. You won't take the truck, but you'll take our clothes?"

"He's taking both, believe me. He knows we can't take the armored car with us, and a nice suit is hard to come by in these parts. Those donkeys are his livelihood. You should be happy he's cutting us such a fair deal."

Clambering atop the fence penning in the livestock—careful to avoid splinters—I selected the healthiest-looking donkey of the lot and slid a leg behind its withers. "This is going to chafe," I mumbled, grabbing hold of the frayed rope leading to the animal's harness.

"Well, if nothing else, this'll make one hell of a story, Cogar," Kailas said, smoothing his plaid boxer shorts as he clambered atop his mount.

"Hey, I thought you were afraid of horses," I said, recalling the fuss he'd made back at the Sabbagh Estate.

"I am. But this isn't a horse. It's a donkey. They're smaller, and they make funny noises. Totally different deal."

I opened my mouth to speak and then closed it without saying a word. It didn't matter that it was a ridiculous distinction to make as long as it got us one step closer to escaping the country.

Patting his donkey's head between its ears, Kailas said, "Anyway, since you've had ten months to take notes and do hands-on research, I expect that this story you're going to write for the *Herald* will be Pulitzer-grade."

"I don't know. They confiscated my phone, my voice recorder, that fancy Nikon SLR you gave me, and my notes a few weeks into my stay. When I insisted that I was a journalist and I needed those things, they scrounged a 10-cent binder of lined paper for me. It's all I've had to work with." I tossed him the ratty notebook.

"You've kept all your notes in this?" Kailas asked as he flipped through. "Each page is missing its bottom half."

"That's also been my only source of toilet paper. I've been forced to write small," I said, shivering as a breeze blew up my shorts.

"That's got to be one of the first times I've heard of a journalist wiping their ass with their own work—usually they leave that to the readers," Kailas said as he broke into laughter—the booming, authentic kind I seldom heard from him.

"Glad to see you haven't lost your sense of humor in all this, old boy," I said with a high-British accent.

"Per mare, per terram, we must carry on, old chap. Screw on your pith helmet, you old poodle-faker, and let's sally forth," Kailas replied in kind, spurring his donkey toward the horizon. I glanced down at the ragged notebook in my hand. Carved deep in the cardboard cover were the lines,

He is one of the Legion Lost;
He was never meant to win;
He's a rolling stone, and it's bred in the bone;
He's a man who won't fit in.

I tore the cover free from its binding and let it flutter to the muddy earth. With a click of my tongue and a tap of my heels against my mount's belly, I set out after Kailas. Together, a fearless two-man cavalcade, we headed straight on into the blinding glow of a new day.

Beauty in the Darkness: One Man's Quest for Understanding in the Syrian Conflict

By Grant Cogar

ALEPPO—It was never my intention to stay in Syria. I left the United States with the same expectations I have of any assignment. Syria was a war zone. Rebels were fighting back against an authoritarian regime. Simple. I'd be in and out of the country within a week or two. But it's never that easy. I found instead a quagmire of religious and socio-political forces battling for control of the country. Each time I attempted to put pen to paper, I found myself frustrated, scratching out lines of text as I tried to formulate a concise means of conveying what was happening here. Because it's not just a war between rebels and a dictator. It may have started out that way, but it's evolved into much more. Weeks turned to months, and it didn't become any easier for me to write this article. Like a holographic billboard, the conflict appeared completely different to those looking at it from each perspective. There's been no reconciling this.

On the religious front, Shi'ite Muslims, including those from Iran and the Lebanese militant group Hezbollah, have flocked to Syria to defend President Assad, an Alawite. Saudi-backed Sunni Muslims, with ties to the known terrorist organization al-Qaeda and other extremist religious forces like the Muslim Brotherhood, have thrown in with the moderates fighting for the Free Syrian Army in hopes of overthrowing Assad and creating a Pan-Islamic state under Sharia law, reinstating the Islamic Caliphate. Toss some Kurdish dissidents in for flavor, and you've got a recipe for full-blown chaos.

Assad, meanwhile, has been working tirelessly to keep his enemies from establishing a foothold, carpeting residential areas under enemy control with barrel bombs dropped from helicopters and firing SCUD missiles and artillery into those neighborhoods before sending in his paid gangs of loyalist militiamen—armed with machetes and an unquenchable bloodlust.

On the sidelines, power players such as the U.S., Russia, Saudi Arabia, and Iran, wage a proxy war—each with their own selfish reasons for hoping the other side loses, jockeying for advantage on the diplomatic stage while funneling weapons and resources to their chosen side.

There's one thing that becomes very evident when looking at these facts: Almost none of the participating factions actually care about Syria itself, though all of them would claim otherwise. Hundreds of thousands of civilians have been killed or forced from the country, and are viewed merely as collateral damage or a necessary sacrifice for a greater cause. Those who fight to regain control of their country in effort to bring about peace are lost to the crowds of foreign militants shouting "*Allahu Akbar!*" as they cut the still-beating hearts from their enemies' chests.

Ten months after arriving in Syria, I can say that I've only unearthed one indisputable fact: There is no good outcome possible in the Syrian Civil War. If Assad wins, the rebels and their supporters will be put to death and his authoritarian dictatorship will continue; the U.S. will have egg on their face while Hezbollah, Iran, and Russia laugh at our incompetence. If the rebels succeed in overcoming Assad, what's left of the country—and there isn't much—will fragment into sectarian violence and undoubtedly account for more deaths than there've been already. Syria will be shattered

and damned to violent fighting for the foreseeable future.

This all seems terribly depressing and hopeless, emotions that weigh heavily upon me even as I write this. But there's beauty hidden away amidst all this deplorable violence, revealed if you scratch away the filth on its surface. Though Syria was a hell unlike any I'd seen, there were still those that walked amidst the bloodshed with pure motive. Free Syrian Army soldiers giving the few crusts of food they had to starving kittens they'd rescued. Kurdish women fighters, standing proudly alongside their male comrades, recalling the Syria they once knew—at one time a thriving, beautiful place. The blind child who held my hand in the darkness of a bullet-riddled orphanage, not because she was scared, but because I was falling apart.

These are things of immense splendor, true and beautiful portrayals of humankind's best side made only more striking by their contrast with the fiery intensity of the war surrounding them. Like these good people lost in the fog of war, we must remember to cling to our humanity, more during these times of strife and insecurity than any other.

Novels aren't just written, they're constructed. Like erecting a building, it takes a raft of very talented craftsmen to bring a project to fruition. I'd like to extend a heartfelt 'thank you' to the following people:

Traci Granzow - Keeper of the household in the mental and physical absence of writer husband

Melanie Granzow - Cheerleader of writer dad

Kevin Granzow - Maker of jaw-dropping cover art and promotional material

Zayne Amer - Worldly traveler who provided translations

Ross Elder - Dulcet tones of the book trailer's narration

Jack Murphy - Pithy international relations advisor

Anastasia Olashaya-Grill – Copy editor extraordinaire

The Gateway Writers Group (Tracey Kelley, Matt Snyder, Chad Cox, Thad Smull), the Skype Squad (Steven Hildreth Jr., Benjamin Cheah, Brian Kunimasa Murata), and Bob Hunter - Editors, beta readers, sounding board, and psychological support team

An outdoorsman, novelist, and journalist, Nate Granzow graduated from Drake University with degrees in English writing and magazine journalism. His work has been published in over 10 professional publications to date, and he currently works as a magazine editor in Des Moines, Iowa.

His debut novel, "The Scorpion's Nest," was selected as one of 1,000 finalists in Amazon's Breakthrough Novel Awards, 2012, and was ranked first in the Mystery/Suspense/Thriller category at the IndieReader Discovery Awards, 2012. His sophomore work, "Cogar's Despair," reached top 100 bestseller status in Amazon's 'Men's Adventure' category, followed by "Cogar's Revolt"—a top three finalist in Clive Cussler Collector's Society's 2014 Adventure Writer's Competition.

A pharmaceutical research facility in the heart of Venezuela's Amazon Basin goes silent without warning. Primordial beasts never before seen by human eyes annihilate the team sent to investigate. Human eyes. The creatures have human eyes. When a newly discovered, but exceedingly rare plant specie shows promise as a possible cure for cancer, pilot Austin Stewart is ordered to accompany the alluring biologist Olivia Dover and her team of researchers to retrieve another specimen. But as the expedition journeys into the rainforest's shadowy depths, they quickly find themselves hunted by the same creatures that slaughtered the rescue team years before—beasts the local Yanomami tribesmen call *hekura*. Evil spirits. But these are no mere apparitions. The research team, forsaken by those that sent them and racing against a Colombian drug lord to recover the precious catholicon, must fight for survival against ravenous mutants too strong to overpower, too intelligent to outsmart. The jungle guards its secrets fiercely.

Find it at nategranzow.com

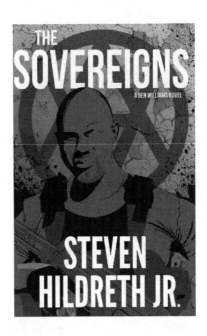

Cogar guest stars in this new release by author Steven Hildreth Jr.

April 17th, 2005. Tucson, Arizona. Led by a charismatic figure identifying himself as "Colonel Rothbard," a militant anarcho-capitalist group known only as the Liberty Brigade has seized control of the Saguaro Towers, taking over a hundred hostages and wiring the buildings with high explosive. Their demands: the United States government has ten hours to bring an end to interventionism overseas, or the towers will be destroyed. But not everyone trapped inside Saguaro is going down without a fight.

Over the course of a career with the CIA's Special Activities Division, Ben Williams has seen terrorists like Rothbard before. He's seen them die. Surrounded by enemies with allies in short supply, Williams finds himself racing against the clock as the seconds tick down toward the deadline. His only objective: stop the Liberty Brigade at all costs.

Find it at stevenhildreth.com